THE
AMATEUR
GEOLOGIST

THE AMATEUR GEOLOGIST

Explorations and Investigations

by Raymond Wiggers

An Amateur Science Series Book
FRANKLIN WATTS
New York·Chicago·London·Toronto·Sydney

Photographs copyright ©: U.S. Geological Survey: pp. 11 (N.P.Peterson), 70 top left (R.L.Parker); American Museum of Natural History, Library Services: pp. 25 (#69190), 42, 43 (#328172 Logan), 56 top right (#41971), 56 center (#42149 E.O.Hovey), 56 bottom left (#319359 Thane Bierwert), 56 bottom right (#116053), 57 center left (#287825) (both J.Kirschner), 57 center right (#298130 Edward Bailey), 57 bottom (#2A8854), 63 top left (#323249), 63 bottom left (#333068) (all Rota), 63 top right (#297242), 66 top (#297270), 66 center (#297276), 70 top right (#297306), 70 bottom left (#297283), 70 bottom right (#297262) (all Dwight Bental); Raymond Wiggers: pp. 27, 29, 30, 33, 63 bottom right; Mike Mogil: p. 31; Photo Researchers: pp. 56 top left (M.Claye Jacana), 57 top right (Roberto DeGugliemo); Color-Pic/E.R. Degginger: p. 57 top left.

Library of Congress Cataloging-in-Publication Data

Wiggers, Raymond.
The amateur geologist : explorations and investigations / by Raymond Wiggers.
p.   cm.—(An Amateur science series book)
Includes bibliographical references and index.
Summary: Presents projects and activities that explore many aspects of the science of geology.
ISBN 0-531-11112-1
1. Geology—Juvenile literature. [1.Geology. 2. Science projects.]
I. Title. II. Series.
QE29.W475   1993
550—dc20
93-13392 CIP AC

Contents

THE
AMATEUR
GEOLOGIST

An Invitation to Explore

To learn about geology is to embark on one of the most exciting journeys possible. On this journey, you will uncover surprising secrets from common, everyday objects and places. Your curiosity will be well rewarded. A small pebble or rock will tell you a story that stretches back millions of years. Your own local area—its hills or plains or waterways—will offer you unexpected clues to the way our whole world came into being.

In fact, one of the best aspects of geology is that you can unlock many of its most exciting wonders without complicated, expensive equipment or extensive training. As an *amateur geologist*, you can conduct your own investigations at home or at school, and there make some of the greatest discoveries the field of earth science has to offer.

In this section, we'll begin the grand adventure with three short explorations designed to get you started as an amateur geologist. The first will acquaint you with a river in your region and will show you how this river has played a major role in shaping the land. The second will send you on a collecting trip to a shoreline or a sandy bank near your home, and it will demonstrate how the river's influence extends far beyond its own boundaries. Then the third exploration will show you how the geologic forces visible in river and shoreline have contributed to our greater understanding of the earth's amazing past.

AMATEUR GEOLOGIST
EXPLORATION NUMBER ONE:
MAPPING A RIVER

The science of geology contains many fascinating subjects and specialties. Some professional geologists spend most of their careers indoors, in laboratories where they analyze rock samples and fossils, or interpret data from satellites and sophisticated ground sensors. Other geologists spend much of their time under the open sky, looking for interesting rock formations or land features that tell them more about the region they're studying. Geologists refer to these outdoor investigations as *fieldwork*, or as being *out in the field.*

An an amateur geologist, you'll find your investigations require a combination of fieldwork and indoor study. This book will give you helpful ideas for both. In the case of this first exploration, though, you don't have to venture outdoors. For equipment you'll need a pencil, a piece of tracing paper, and a road or atlas map of your own state. (You can get inexpensive tracing paper at your local art or office supplier, and suitable maps are sold at gas stations and convenience stores.)

When you're ready to start, open up the map and find the largest river in your own area. At first it may be a little hard to follow the river's course, because of all the town names and roads printed next to it, but if you're careful you won't lose track of it.

Believe it or not, this river is a goldmine of information. For example, you'll find that it is connected to a network of smaller rivers or brooks that connect with still others. All these smaller streams that feed the main river are *tributaries* (Figure 1-1).

Geologists call this overall pattern of a river and its tributaries a *drainage net.* Let's see what the drainage net in your state really looks like. Place tracing paper on top of the map, so that the map is clearly visible through

Figure 1–1. An aerial view of a drainage net, Gila County, Arizona. A study of water flow can tell you much about the topography of a region.

the paper. Use your pencil to copy the course of the main river, as far as you can. Then trace its tributaries, too, making sure they connect with the big river at the right places.

Now lift the tracing paper off the map. It may look something like Figure 1-2. Does the drainage net you've drawn have a shape that reminds you of anything? Does it look like a tree, a web, or a ladder? Can you tell which way the water flows, just from looking at the pattern?

While other shapes are possible, many drainage nets do look like the branching of a tree. The smallest tributaries resemble the tree's outermost twigs, and from there the branches get bigger and bigger till they reach the trunk, the main river.

It probably won't surprise you to learn that the water in a drainage system always flows downhill. That means the smallest, most distant streams are on higher ground

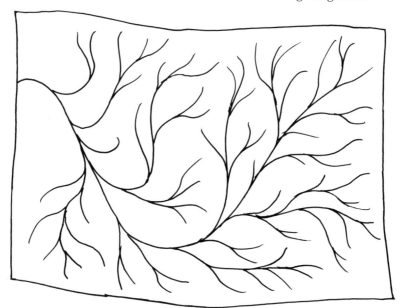

Figure 1-2. *Your own drainage net tracing might look like this.*

than the bigger tributaries, and in turn the bigger tributaries are on higher ground than the main river. So by just looking at a map, you can see which way the land slopes, even if the map doesn't show any hills or mountains.

Before we finish this first exploration, let's consider what the drainage net actually does. Of course, it carries water from higher places to a lower place, such as a lake or the sea. But is that all? Do rivers and their streams do anything else?

In fact, the drainage net you've discovered is one of the most powerful forces acting on your region's landscape. Rain falling in the upland areas picks up and moves particles of disintegrating rock and carries them into the nearest stream. From there the particles move— in the form of silt, sand, gravel, and larger stones—into the big river. Over the course of thousands of years, huge quantities of these particles, or *sediments,* are transported downhill, all the way to the ocean or some other large body of water. As more sediments are washed away, the land upstream gets flatter and flatter. In an even longer time period, in millions of years, entire mountain ranges can totally disappear.

This process of moving sediments from high areas to low places is known as *erosion.* Erosion on this scale wouldn't be possible without rivers, so you can see how important they are in changing the shape and height of the land. But what about those sediments that were carried away? Can we still find some lingering trace of them? That's the purpose of our second exploration.

AMATEUR GEOLOGIST
EXPLORATION NUMBER TWO:
A TRIP TO THE BEACH

This time our investigation does take us outdoors—to a beach on a pond, lake or seacoast in your area. The goal of the trip is simple enough: to collect a sample of

13

sediments. If you don't live near a beach, you can try your local stream or river; gravel, sand, and clay deposits can often be found along the banks. Remember to be extra careful, though, and collect a sample only where it's permitted. *In any case, never collect sediments from an area that isn't both clean and safe.* Be especially certain that your material doesn't contain any unwanted debris, such as broken glass, refuse, or decaying matter.

For this investigation, you'll need just three basic items: a tall glass or plastic jar with a screw lid, a shallow baking pan, and a magnifying glass. Of these, the only thing you'll have to take to the beach is the jar.

When you get to the beach or streambank, find a good sampling location and fill a quarter to a third of your jar with sediments from a location near the water's edge. For best results, try to get a mixture of small pebbles, sand, and clay or mud. Before you return home, take a look around. How do you think the sediments you collected got there in the first place? Is there any evidence that the water played any role in the process?

Once you're back home, fill the rest of the jar with tap water. Screw the lid on tightly and shake the container vigorously till the sediments are well mixed with the water. Then set the jar down on a shelf or table and watch how the sediments settle to the bottom. Which type of sediment settles out first? Is it the extremely fine clay or mud particles, the medium-sized sand grains, or the pebbles larger than the sand? If you have a good mixture, you should eventually see a pattern similar to what you see in Figure 1-3.

Next, gently drain the water out of the jar and spread the sediments out onto the baking pan. Make doubly sure that any bits of flammable material such as paper are removed, then place the pan (uncovered) into your kitchen oven preheated to 500° F. By letting the sample "cook" for about 30 minutes you'll help to sterilize it and also make sure it's completely dry, so the grains won't stick together. When you remove the pan from

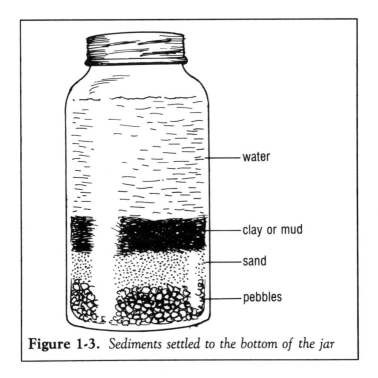

Figure 1-3. *Sediments settled to the bottom of the jar*

the oven, let it cool in an out-of-the-way place. One word of warning: the sediments will probably remain hot much longer than the pan does!

Now you are ready to examine your sample. You may be surprised how much you can learn from it. First of all, stand back a few feet from it and decide what overall color it is. Then look at it more closely. Are all the particles the same color, or are some darker and some lighter? Are any of the particles black, or pink, or shiny, or glassy?

Next, use your magnifying glass to look at the particles in still greater detail. Are they round or flat or needle-shaped? Are their edges sharp or smooth? This is the kind of question geologists ask in order to find out where the sand came from, and to learn more about the sampling location itself.

Fortunately, we don't need to do the kind of detailed analysis the experts do. We've already seen enough to get a good idea of the sediments' "life story." Regardless of where you collected it, the chances are that it's composed of quite an array of different particles. Some are larger than others; some have one type of shape, and others, another. And it's very likely that you'll find that the colors of the grains vary, too.

In fact, these different kinds of particles are tiny bits of stone and minerals that have been washed up to your sampling site by the motion of the water. In some cases, they come from rock formation or older sediment deposits eroding by the edge of the lake or sea. But they may also have come from even farther away, from rocks on a hillside or bluff many miles more distant. How did they manage to travel that far?

To answer that, all you have to do is think back to our first exploration, where we discovered that the land is worn away by erosion. Sediments, including the sand you collected, are eventually washed downhill by streams. Some of the sediments come to rest in deposits along the creeks and rivers, and some are carried all the way to the main river's end, at a lake or sea.

Once in the larger body of water, some of the sediments are carried by powerful shoreline currents and deposited on beaches. If you collected your sand at a beach, those currents were your sample's "delivery service." But still other sediments are taken farther out. They begin to settle, and quickly or slowly they come to rest on the bottom, where they lie buried in layer after layer. In some places these deposits are thousands of feet deep.

In the course of millions of years the layers of buried sediments are once more formed into rock. Each kind of sediment becomes its own distinctive kind of rock, which often differs in color or texture from the layers surrounding it. Each of these many layers can be thought of as a single chapter in a very long book.

One of the first and most exciting discoveries of the early geologists was that many of the layered rocks we see on land were once at the bottom of ancient, long-vanished lakes and seas. For a variety of reasons—everything from violent upheaval in the earth's crust to a gentle lowering of sea level—these rocks became exposed on dry land, after lying submerged for millions of years.

In unlocking the secrets of the rocks, scientists made a simple but incredibly important discovery: *the individual layers could be "read," as though they were chapters in a book, with the deepest layers representing the book's earliest chapters.* As long as the rock hadn't been tilted, bent, or toppled, the lowest layers were oldest, and the highest layers were youngest. Once that was understood, geologists realized they could also determine the age of rocks in their own region by comparing them to the patterns of rock layers elsewhere.

That is one of the ways we now know a good deal about our planet's past. And our planet's past, with all its drama, is where our third and final journey will take us.

AMATEUR GEOLOGIST EXPLORATION NUMBER THREE: THE GEOLOGIC TIMESCALE

When over 300 years ago scientists did start to compare the patterns of rock layers from many places, they were actually beginning to construct a sort of "planetary calendar," made up of many significant points in the earth's long history. Before this calendar was put together, most people assumed that the world—and even the universe as a whole—were only a few thousand years old. In this exploration, however, we'll follow in the footsteps of the geologists who first learned how ancient our earth truly is.

While normal calendars are subdivided into months and weeks, the planetary calendar, usually called the *geologic timescale,* consists of sections called *eras* and *periods.* But whereas months and weeks are made up of days—a length of time we can all understand—the eras and periods of geologists are made up of millions, or even billions, of years.

To get a better feeling for the incredible length of the earth's history, you can construct your own version of the geologic timescale. To do this, you'll need a ruler, a total of eleven sheets of blank notebook paper ($8\frac{1}{2}$ by 11 inches), a regular black-ink pen, and colored pencils or markers in the following colors: blue, yellow, red, and green.

When you're ready, tape the eleven sheets of paper together, so they're connected end to end. Do this as neatly as you can, to prevent puckering. The result will be one continuous sheet of paper. Next, use your ruler and black pen to draw a very long and narrow rectangle on the sheet. This rectangle should measure 6 inches wide by 10 feet long.

Now lay your ruler along the bottom edge of the rectangle, so that the ruler's inch scale starts exactly at the right-hand corner. Then mark the rectangle's bottom line lightly at the following points: at 2 inches from the right corner, at 6 inches from the right corner, and at 15 inches from the right corner. Then use the ruler to make exactly the same marks on the rectangle's upper edge, and draw a line between each pair of marks— from the upper 2-inch mark to the lower 2-inch mark, and so on.

Without realizing it, you've already determined the eras of the geologic timescale. To make the eras more apparent, color the section of the rectangle from the righthand edge to the 2-inch line green, the section from 2 to 6 inches red, the section from 6 to 15 inches yellow, and the very large remaining section on the left, blue. The result should look something like Figure 1-4.

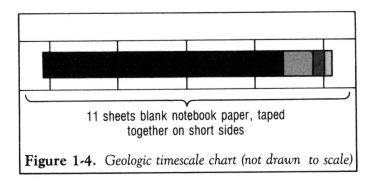

11 sheets blank notebook paper, taped
together on short sides

Figure 1-4. *Geologic timescale chart (not drawn to scale)*

Now label each era with its "official" geologic name. The big blue section is *Precambrian time;* the yellow is the *Paleozoic Era;* the red is the *Mesozoic Era;* the green is the *Cenozoic Era.* Each of these eras is composed of smaller periods, and each of these also has its own name. We'll learn more about some of those later on in this book.

The most obvious thing about the geologic timescale you've made is that the eras are all different sizes. The blue Precambrian is by far the largest—and this makes good sense when you realize that this span of almost 9 feet lasted for almost 4 billion years! This first and longest chapter of the earth's history began with the formation of the earth out of the dust and debris that circled our young sun. Only about a quarter of the Precambrian had passed before the miracle of life—in the form of tiny single-celled creatures—had begun.

Not until the next era, the yellow Paleozoic, did the ancestors of the kinds of larger plants and animals we know today appear in great abundance. In the Paleozoic—which lasted somewhat more than 300 million years—the forms of life on earth became staggeringly diverse, from fishes and many other creatures in the seas, to the plants, insects, and amphibians that first colonized the land.

The red Mesozoic Era (roughly 160 million years) is better known by another name, the Age of Reptiles,

19

even though those creatures weren't the only wonders of that time. For the world was also transformed by the rise of the flowering plants, which brought a vast increase of color and variety to the earth's surface.

The final era, the Cenozoic, is often nicknamed "the Age of Mammals," even though the earliest mammals came into being long before this time. The Cenozoic is our current era; since it has only run for about 65 million years so far, it has a long way to go before it matches any of the other eras in length.

Looking at the simple timescale you've constructed, you can make some amazing discoveries. We've already noted the most obvious point, that the first era, the Precambrian, is much bigger than the others (it is even much larger than the three others combined!). Think about that. Remembering that the Precambrian was the era before the arrival of most many-celled organisms, what conclusions can you draw?

For one thing, it shows the more complex life-forms—such as fish, insects, reptiles, and trees—are actually latecomers in the story of life, no matter how ancient they may appear to us. Though many of their forms are now extinct, all these creatures came into being only *after* the Precambrian—which made up almost nine tenths of the earth's history—had ended.

Next, take a look at the Mesozoic era, the time when the dinosaurs held sway. It's true that it didn't last as long as either the Precambrian or the Paleozoic, but it was still considerably longer than our own era, the Cenozoic. This demonstrates that the dinosaurs, far from being unsuccessful, primitive animals (as they are still sometimes portrayed) survived and thrived for well over 150 million years. In contrast, we human beings have been on earth for *less than 1 percent* of that span!

And that humbling fact brings us to the one important thing our geologic timescale can't show. The entire length of human history, *in geologic terms*, simply isn't big enough to be seen at the end of the calendar. The whole story of humankind—from its origin in Africa through the rise and fall of many civilizations—fits within the single pen line that bounds the rectangle on the far right. This humbling fact teaches us the true scale of time.

Keep the lessons of these first three explorations in mind as you continue through this book. The ideas we've covered will help you with your further investigations as an amateur geologist. Now that you recognize some of the great forces that shape the land, and better understand the vast scale of time, you hold a key that opens the door to the exciting science of geology, and the history of the earth.

How to Be an Amateur Geologist

More than anything else, being an amateur geologist means being observant. As we learned in the explorations in Chapter One, everyday sights and objects often tell us more than they seem to. By paying attention to the world around us, we can make important discoveries that otherwise would elude us.

Of course, it's important to know *how* to be observant—and for that you'll have to know what to look for and where to look; also, you will need to know what tools and other equipment will help you be an effective geological explorer. That's the purpose of this chapter.

WHAT TO LOOK FOR

What sorts of things should an amateur geologist look for? What kinds of places are most likely to give the best clues and evidence in your geological sleuthing? You may be surprised at the number and variety of places that will reward your curiosity. Here are some ideas to set you on the right path; later on, as you gain experience, you'll be able to find many others, all on your own.

1. Your Own Home Turf • Some of the best discoveries in earth science lie waiting for you in your own neighborhood. It may not seem so at first, but wherever there is a rock-strewn vacant lot, an eroding stream gully, or a building surfaced with granite or limestone, there is some fascinating aspect of geology that cries out for understanding. And don't forget such precious resources as your school and town libraries. Even the most modest collection of science books may contain priceless information and ideas that can transport your imagination, if not your physical self, to the flanks of erupting volcanoes and the crevasses of huge Arctic glaciers.

2. Museums and Other Indoor Geologic Exhibits • One of the best places to start studying the geology of your area is at a natural history museum (Figure 2-1). Many major cities (New York, Chicago, and Denver, to name a few) have such institutions, but they're not just found in the biggest urban centers. Many universities and community colleges have nature museums; in fact, it's even possible that your local high school, public library, or town hall has its own display of rocks, fossils, or minerals painstakingly assembled by amateur geologists like you. Visiting these "indoor resources" is an excellent way to prepare for your later expeditions. Appendix A lists some of America's most significant geology museums and related exhibits.

3. Parks and Vacation Areas • Many places of outstanding natural significance have been turned into national parks, monuments, or seashores, which are visited by millions of people each year. Most of these are prime geology sites where a great deal of exciting information on earth history is available. Many state-run facilities preserve locations that are just as interesting, and in some cases city and town parks contain their own wonders worthy of a geologist's scrutiny. In New York City, for instance, Central Park has rock formations half a billion years old, some of which still bear scratches from Ice Age glaciers. (For the names of national and state park sites of special interest to geologists, see Appendix A.)

Figure 2–1. The American Museum of Natural History in New York City. A visit to a geology exhibit in your region will help to prepare you for fieldwork.

4. Rock Outcrops and Roadcuts • Rock outcrops are locations where the earth's bedrock—otherwise hidden from view—is exposed to the open air. Outcrops may be composed of differing rock layers which, through their orientation or folding, reveal much about an area's inner structure and the changes that have occurred there over millions of years.

As an amateur geologist you will probably want to visit outcrops and then later study the rock samples you collect there. In addition, some outcrops contain minerals of note, and others may be a rich source of fossils. In some areas of the country, such as the Rocky Mountains, the California seacoast, and New England, rock outcrops are plentiful. In other areas, however, the bedrock is usually buried under layers of soil, glacial debris, or sediments, so that it cannot be seen for miles. This is true, for instance, in many parts of the Midwest. See Appendix A for descriptions of good collecting regions.

Roadcuts are a kind of outcrop that geologists especially like (Figure 2-2). They are formed when a new roadway is excavated through previously buried rock formations. Here field scientists have the chance to see and sample "fresh" rocks before they're covered with mineral staining and vegetation. If your expeditions take you to roadcuts, be extremely careful, and stay well clear of passing vehicles. Also keep in mind that it is generally illegal to stop along interstate highways—where the best roadcuts usually are—except in an emergency.

5. Quarries • In many locations across America stone has been mined in quarries for its commercial value. Granite, marble, and sandstone obtained in this way are frequently used for buildings and monuments, while other types of rock, such as quartzite, may be broken into small pieces and sold for railroad bedding or other construction uses.

Large amounts of rocks are exposed at quarries, so

Figure 2–2. A roadcut into ancient metamorphic rock in northwestern Connecticut. Roadcuts offer unique opportunities to "see inside the earth."

they are often excellent places to learn more about geology. But quarries can also be more dangerous than normal outcrops. At an active quarry (that is, at one that is still being operated) you must obtain permission from the management before you enter it; blasting explosives and heavy machinery may otherwise catch you unaware. On the other hand, inactive or abandoned quarries may be partially flooded or have undermined areas. Whenever possible, check with the owners of the land before you enter the quarry grounds.

6. Inactive Mines and Spoil Piles • Many old and abandoned mines, ranging from small open-air pits to shafts that go deep underground, can be found in various parts of the country. Often mounds of discarded rock, called *spoil piles,* are found near mine entrances; they can be excellent places to hunt for minerals and gemstones.

It is always a wise idea to obtain the landowner's permission before you go exploring on private property, and mines are no exception to that rule. *In addition, you should never enter a mineshaft or pit unless you are accompanied by an adult.* Spoil piles can be hazardous, too: poisonous chemical compounds may be present in, or draining out of, the debris. Play it safe and first check with the local county health department, the police, or your regional office of the Environmental Protection Agency.

7. Landforms • A landform is any feature on the surface of the earth that has been produced by natural forces: mountains, hills, valleys, sand dunes, and plains are all landforms, and the list just begins there (see Figure 2-3, 2-4, and 2-5). Generally speaking, landforms are worth seeing not so much because of their rocks, fossils, or minerals, but because their overall shapes reveal how a region has been affected by such forces as wind, water,

Figure 2–3. An ancient (Silurian Period) coral reef exposed and partially destroyed by the Wasbash River near Lagro, Indiana

Figure 2–4. Mount Hor and Lake Willoughby,
as seen from Mount Pisgah, in northeastern Vermont.
Both the deep lake and steep mountain were
scoured by the advance of Ice Age glaciers.

Figure 2–5. The "two mittens" of Monument Valley, Arizona, are red sandstone monoliths deposited during the Permian Period capped by a Triassic conglomerate more resistant to erosion.

and even landslides, earthquakes, volcanic eruptions, and glaciers.

Unlike outcrops and other rock-sampling sites, landforms are practically everywhere. Even the flattest prairie is a landform, and the careful observer learns that it has its tale to tell. Further, landforms don't have to be gigantic. An animal's burrow is a kind of landform, too, even though it may be just a few inches across.

TOOLS AND OTHER GEAR
YOU MAY NEED

If you wanted to go birdwatching or fishing, you wouldn't get very far if you didn't have binoculars or a rod and reel. To pursue those interests, you have to be properly equipped. In the same way, the amateur geologist needs certain tools and other gear (Figure 2-6). Naturally, what you'll want to take may vary somewhat, depending on your exact interests and on where you're going. However, the following list covers most of the items you will need for your fieldwork, and also for your study at home.

1. Field Equipment • The most common tool of field geologists is the *rock hammer*. As its name implies, it is used to knock or pry rock samples from outcrops. In size and shape it's quite similar to a normal hammer, but it usually has a squared-off front end and a pointed extension, like a pick, on the back. As every veteran rockhound knows, the use of a rock hammer often produces sharp, flying chips of stone that have the potential of blinding a person in an instant. Prevent this serious danger by donning *safety glasses* or other protective eyewear whenever you wield the hammer.

Another important piece of gear is the *hand lens*, a small magnifying glass that is downright essential if you want to examine crystal or fossil details too small to be seen with the naked eye. The best kind of hand lens is

Figure 2–6. *Useful tools to have (left to right): geological rock hammer, triplet hand lens, safety goggles*

designed to be retracted inside a jacket or sheath when not in use, so it won't be scratched accidentally. Next, a small, all-purpose *folding knife* often proves to be a very useful item; and a *biology probe*—a steel point with a wooden handle—is helpful in carefully removing dirt or clay from fossils or other specimens.

If you plan to collect specimens in the field (especially fragile or dusty ones), take along a supply of *sample bags.* Plastic freezer bags with locking tops work well, though heavier samples, such as large rocks, may require sturdier containers—canvas bookbags and the like. (One advantage of bagging all of your samples separately is that you can label and keep track of them more easily.) Also, you will need some sort of *field notebook* in which you can record your observations. Naturally, a dependable *pen* or *pencil* is a must, too. A camera is another useful recording tool.

The more specialized tools mentioned—the rock hammer, safety glasses, hand lens, and biology probe—are available from science suppliers, and also more locally at college bookstores or hardwares. See Appendix C for the names of some of the better known suppliers.

2. Field Information • Once you've decided to visit a geological site, you'll need exact information on how to get there. If you plan to visit a state or national park, a general road map that shows you how to reach it may be enough. There are other, more detailed maps, though; at the very least they will add to your appreciation of a particular location, and sometimes they'll be absolutely essential.

Topographic maps, published by the United States Geological Survey, are available for each section of the country and show the elevations of the land, as well as hills, valleys, rivers, towns, and so on. They are the best way to locate a particular site accurately. In addition there are more specialized *geologic maps* that show the precise location of an area's soils, sediment deposits, or bedrock types. Topographic maps are sold directly by the Geological Survey and by map stores and are also sometimes available from book shops and camping suppliers. Most geologic maps are printed and sold by state geological surveys or environmental agencies.

Special *Geological Highway Maps*, published by the American Association of Petroleum Geologists (known as the AAPG, for short), cover each region of the United States and provide a variety of interesting facts useful to professional and amateur geologists alike. On top of that, some state geological surveys, museum shops, and park and private bookstores offer *printed field trips, road logs,* and *roadside geology* guides. These texts are often written specifically for amateur geologists and are chock full of interesting facts. See Appendix B for more information about the AAPG maps and the other items described in this section.

Finally, *field guides* are another excellent source of information. These portable, easy-to-use books usually cover one particular topic—landforms, for instance, or fossils, rock types, or minerals—and they allow you to match your finds with their identifying pictures or descriptions. They are offered by most good bookstores.

3. More Equipment for Your Home Lab or Workshop • There are a few other items that usually aren't needed in the field but are useful later on, when you begin to study your samples at home. One is the *streak plate,* a piece of unglazed porcelain used to help identify metallic minerals. If you wish to study stream or beach sediments, you may wish to get a set of *graduated sieves* that separate the sediments by particle size. Both sieve sets and streak plates can be ordered from science suppliers, as can *boxed sets* of labeled minerals, rocks, and fossils. While not essential, these minimuseums are terrific learning tools. Not only are they interesting in themselves—they also help you identify specimens you've collected yourself.

Geology
Facts
and
Ideas

Modern geology can be likened to a fancy, dazzling gemstone with many facets. Each of these glittering facets is its own field of scientific inquiry. No one text can cover all these exciting fields, but in this section we will consider some of the most important aspects of earth science—and those best suited to your investigations as an amateur geologist. In short, this part of the book is a reference section designed to stimulate your curiosity, while it answers the most common questions you'll come across in your explorations. You'll also find this section especially helpful when you try the projects described in Chapter Four. In other words, think of this section as a built-in "miniencyclopedia" of geology.

THE GEOLOGIC TIMESCALE AND THE HISTORY OF THE EARTH

In Chapter One we had our first look at the geologic timescale, the "planetary calendar" that shows the earth's history. When you constructed your own timescale, you learned its most basic divisions, the *eras*—the Precambrian, the Paleozoic, the Mesozoic, and the Cenozoic—as well as their relative lengths. Now we delve a little deeper and discover the important events of each era.

First, take a look at the overall geologic timescale shown in Figure 3-1. It resembles the one you made in Chapter One, but it additionally contains dates along

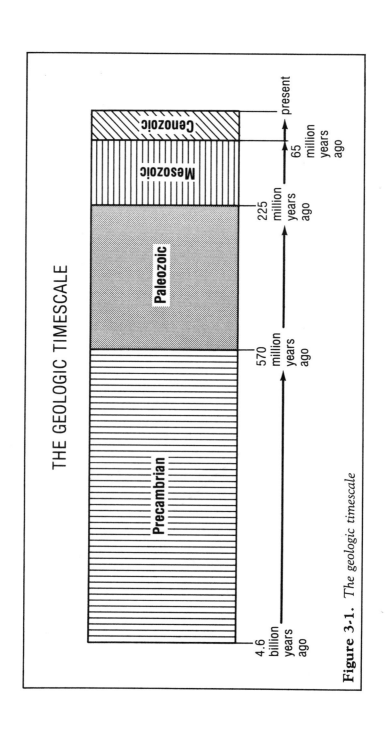

Figure 3-1. *The geologic timescale*

the lower edge of the scale that mark the limits of each era. You'll notice that Precambrian time began at the far left, a mindboggling 4.6 billion years ago, and lasted up to 570 million years before the present. Let's peer into this vast and still largely mysterious gulf of prehistory before we consider the more recent eras.

1. The Precambrian • As mentioned earlier, this era (Figure 3-2) makes up the bulk of all our planet's history. Despite that, we know much less about it than the times that followed, because many of the rock formations and fossils from those early days have disappeared or been altered beyond recognition. Still, we know a few basic, but very exciting, facts.

At about 3.8 billion years, the crust of our good companion, the moon, had formed, even though its great open areas, or *maria*, had yet to be flooded with molten rock. Back on earth, a miraculous thing had happened by 3.5 billion years at the latest: life, in the form of rudimentary bacteria, had come into being. The cells of these earliest creatures were very primitive; an additional 2 billion years passed before other tiny, one-celled beings with a more complex structure appeared. Only after yet another huge span of time did the first forms of life composed of *many* cells find their way into the fossil record, at a point much closer to the end of the Precambrian. Finally the stage was set for the dramatic events that followed.

2. The Paleozoic Era • The word *Paleozoic* comes from two words in the classical Greek language meaning "ancient life"—but as we've seen, the most ancient life of all began far back in the Precambrian. Scientists who study the history of the earth have broken down the Paleozoic and its succeeding eras into smaller parts, called *periods* (Figure 3-3). We'll take a look at each of these in turn, because each period is really a distinct and exciting chapter in the history of life.

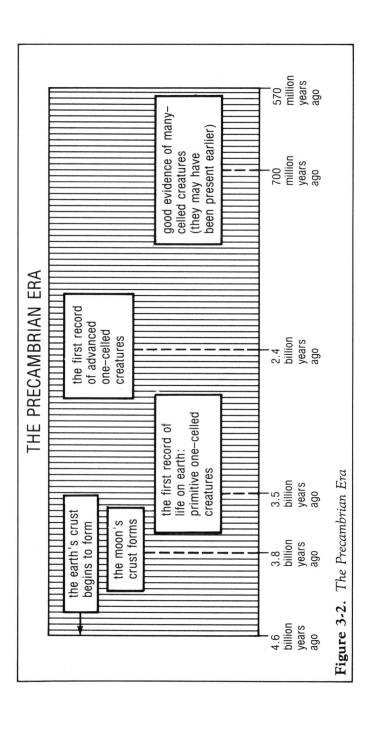

Figure 3-2. *The Precambrian Era*

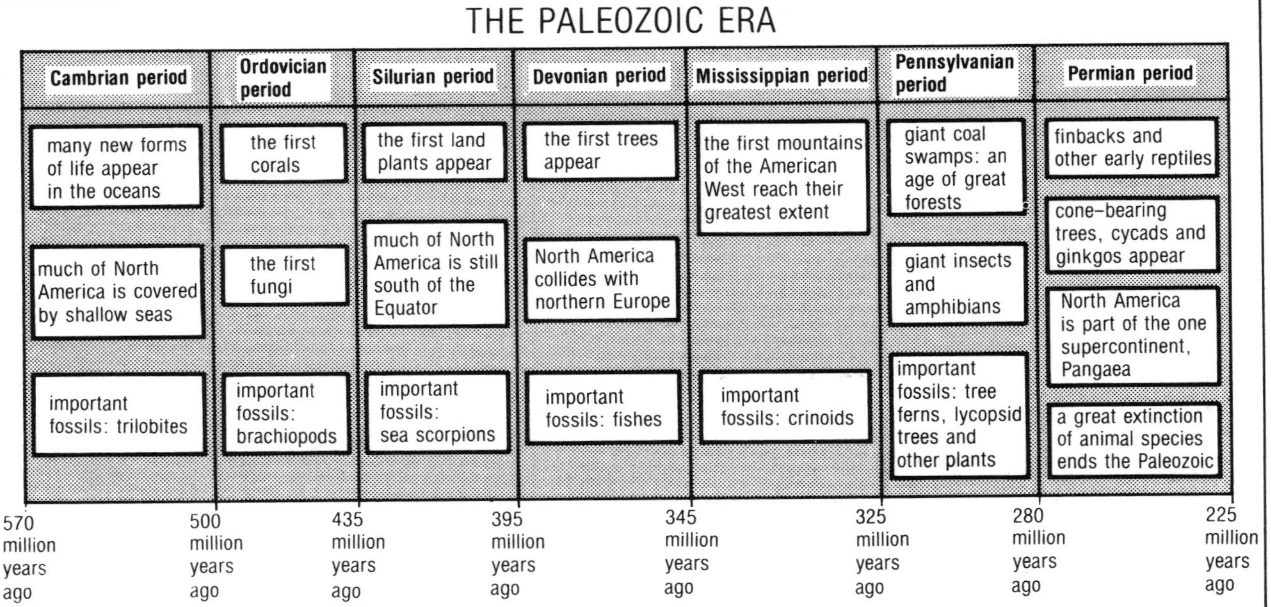

THE PALEOZOIC ERA

Cambrian period	Ordovician period	Silurian period	Devonian period	Mississippian period	Pennsylvanian period	Permian period
many new forms of life appear in the oceans	the first corals	the first land plants appear	the first trees appear	the first mountains of the American West reach their greatest extent	giant coal swamps: an age of great forests	finbacks and other early reptiles
much of North America is covered by shallow seas	the first fungi	much of North America is still south of the Equator	North America collides with northern Europe		giant insects and amphibians	cone-bearing trees, cycads and ginkgos appear
						North America is part of the one supercontinent, Pangaea
important fossils: trilobites	important fossils: brachiopods	important fossils: sea scorpions	important fossils: fishes	important fossils: crinoids	important fossils: tree ferns, lycopsid trees and other plants	a great extinction of animal species ends the Paleozoic

570 million years ago — 500 million years ago — 435 million years ago — 395 million years ago — 345 million years ago — 325 million years ago — 280 million years ago — 225 million years ago

Figure 3-3. *The Paleozoic Era*

The first period of the Paleozoic was the *Cambrian*, which lasted from 570 to 500 million years ago. Here, at last, the record of life truly blossomed. Early in the Cambrian we find creatures of many different designs—some quite familiar, others so bizarre that they seem to have been invented by an extremely imaginative science-fiction writer. Before long, however, this great diversity of life-forms gave way to a smaller variety of basic patterns. The creatures that followed fit within those fewer basic patterns, then expanded in number, in a sort of population explosion, to fill many new environments.

The Cambrian Period was also a time when the early version of our continent, North America, was covered by warm, shallow seas. One of the most prevalent kinds of animal inhabiting these seas was the *trilobite*. Trilobite fossils are often found in rock formations of Cambrian age.

The second Paleozoic period was the *Ordovician;* it lasted from 500 to 435 million years ago. Among the new arrivals then were reef-building corals and the humble but crucially important fungi. Two types of marine fossils especially common in Ordovician rocks are *graptolites*, with strange tube- or branch-shaped remains, and *brachiopods;* beautiful shelled creatures resembling clams, but actually not closely related to them.

The next period, running from 435 to 395 million years ago, was the *Silurian*. Before its end the first plants had appeared on land. In the open waters or lagoons of this time were giant *sea scorpions*, some over 9 feet in length, and even more formidable than their modern-day land-scorpion descendants. Meanwhile, much of ancestral North America was actually located *south* of the equator. Like the various forms of life that now swarmed on and around them, the continents themselves were moving, evolving, and changing their appearance in every period.

The *Devonian,* which followed, was a good example of how much the continents could move across the earth's surface (see Figure 3-4). During this period, from 395 to 345 million years ago, the ocean between northern Europe and eastern North America slowly closed, and the two landmasses collided. As we'll see, this episode of crashing continents was by no means the last. At the same time, the first trees were growing to heights of 30 or 40 feet, and armored fishes called *placoderms* replaced their more primitive counterparts, and so ruled the ocean depths. Indeed, they were so successful that the Devonian is often known as the Age of the Fishes.

By the *Mississippian* (345 to 325 million years ago), the first known mountain range in western North America had reared its head, in what is now the Nevada area. It was in this period that odd-looking animals known as *crinoids* were very common in the oceans.

The *Pennsylvanian,* from 325 to 280 million years ago, was the time of the great coal swamps. Huge tracts of ancient forests stretched for hundreds of miles across much of our continent, and time and again the sea invaded this flat, lush lowland. A vast quantity of plant debris was produced by these swamps. Later, when it was buried by layers of sediments, it gradually turned into the dark, compact substance we call coal. (Most of the coal mined in the United States comes from these Pennsylvanian deposits). *Seed ferns, lycopsids,* and other primitive trees towered over a vast array of smaller plants while amphibians and giant insects—including 4-inch cockroaches and dragonflies with 3-foot wingspans—held sway in this wet and leafy world.

Things were very different, though, in the last period of the Paleozoic, the *Permian.* By this point all the earth's wayward continents had joined into one great landmass. The waterlogged conditions of the Pennsylvanian gave way to arid, perhaps even desertlike, climates in many parts of the globe. In this setting a new

Figure 3–4. *Artist's depiction of a forest of the Devonian Period*

kind of land animal, the reptile, became dominant. This was the time of *Dimetrodon* and the other great fin-backed beasts that flourished millions of years before the first dinosaur. At the very end of the Permian, however, one of the most baffling events in our planet's history took place—a mass extinction, in which many species of animals, as well as some plant types, were swept out of existence in a relatively short span.

Experts still aren't sure what caused this extinction and the others that have occurred at regular intervals in the story of life, but one thing is clear: The disaster that ended the Paleozoic era was immense. According to some researchers, from 50 to 90 percent of all types of living beings perished. The next era would begin with a slate wiped almost clean.

3. The Mesozoic Era • *Mesozoic* means "middle life," because scientists originally thought this era was the middle part of earth history. (Take another look at our modern version of the geologic timescale in Figure 3-1. You'll see that the Mesozoic is much closer to our own time than it is to the real midpoint). Most people know this era by its popular nickname, the Age of Reptiles. But this marvelous and diverse group of animals was only one of the wonders that appeared in the three periods of the Mesozoic (see Figure 3-5).

The first of these periods was the *Triassic* (225 to 195 million years ago). As you'll recall, a great extinction had taken place at the end of the preceding Permian Period. So Triassic forms of life were the descendents of the lucky survivors of that disaster. Among the new land animals were the early dinosaurs; in the sea, coil-shelled relatives of the modern squid, known as *ammonites*, became prevalent and remained so till the very end of the Mesozoic Era.

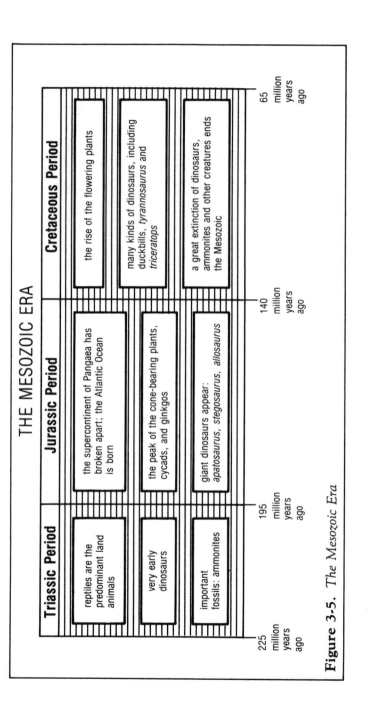

Figure 3·5. *The Mesozoic Era*

By the end of the Triassic the shape of the land was changing again. For 50 million years, and perhaps even longer, a single landmass had stretched from the North Pole to the South—a vast, united supercontinent in the one great sea. But cracks were appearing. For instance, the east coast of America was beginning to split away from northwestern Africa. And so it was that the modern Atlantic Ocean was born as the next period, the *Jurassic,* dawned.

The Jurassic lasted from 195 to 140 million years ago. It was the time of *Archaeopterix,* the famous ancestor of modern birds, and of such giant dinosaurs as the formidably armed plant-eating *Stegosaurus,* the meat-eating *Allosaurus,* and the massive *Apatosaurus* (which is still better known by its old name of *Brontosaurus*). These animals occupied environments filled with fascinating and often strange-looking trees, including cycads, ginkgos, and *conifers* (cone-bearing plants in the same group as our modern pines and spruces). These kinds of plants are still with us to some extent, but the Jurassic was definitely their heyday. In the final period of the Mesozoic, the *Cretaceous,* they would be pushed into the background, so to speak, by a quiet but far-reaching revolution.

That revolution was the sudden rise of modern plants. Previously, most plants had reproduced by being pollinated and by making seeds, but they did so in a relatively clumsy, wasteful way. But the new Cretaceous plants arrived on the scene equipped with an amazing "reproduction machine" never seen before—the flower. Unlike their earlier counterparts, such later dinosaurs as *Tyrannosaurus* and *Triceratops* shared the world with blooming magnolias, fig trees, and oaks, and also with butterflies and bees, which owed their very existence to the new flowers.

The Mesozoic Era ended the same way the Paleozoic had, with the disappearance of many forms of life. This time, the chief victims were the great dinosaurs and the ammonites and other marine animals. There are many theories that seek to explain this extinction, from the impact of a large meteorite to continental drift, changing climates, and shifting ocean currents. Whatever the cause really was, the flowering plants weathered the crisis well and went on to make our planet greener than it had ever been before.

4. The Cenozoic Era • Finally we reach our own era, the shortest; its name means "recent life." Also called the Age of the Mammals, the Cenozoic is split into just two periods, which in turn are subdivided into several *epochs* (Figure 3-6).

The first of the two periods, the *Tertiary*, was by far the longest: it stretched from the end of the Cretaceous, 65 million years ago, to just 2 million years before the present. The Tertiary is made up of five epochs: the oldest was the *Paleocene;* it was followed by the *Eocene, Oligocene, Miocene,* and *Pliocene.*

Truth to tell, mammals first appeared in the fossil record long before the onset of the Tertiary, but it was in this period that they clearly rose to predominance. It was also boom times for the rapidly developing flowering plants. Among these, the grasses became widespread for the first time, and a carpet of vegetation spread across many parts of the earth as never before. Meanwhile the Atlantic Ocean continued to widen. North America was well above the equator, not far from its current location. By the end of the Tertiary, the Rocky Mountains were given a new lease on life, as the western side of our continent was slowly but surely pushed upward, far above sea level.

And that brings us to our own brief period, the *Quaternary*, which is only a scant 2 million years old. It is composed of just two epochs, the *Pleistocene* and the *Holocene* (which is sometimes called the *Recent* instead). The Quaternary is a tiny slice of time, geologi-

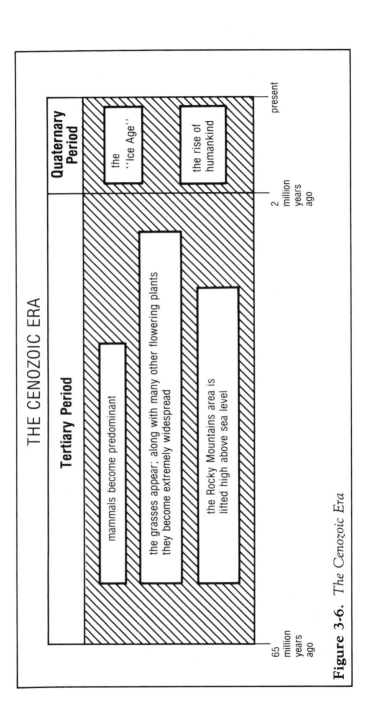

Figure 3-6. *The Cenozoic Era*

cally speaking, but it has been chock-full of unusual events. In this latest episode of our earth's history gigantic ice sheets from the northern polar region moved far south, only to eventually retreat again, in at least four major episodes. This is what we know as the Ice Age—when New England, New York, much of the Midwest, and parts of the Far West (not to mention much of northern Europe and parts of Asia) were buried by blankets of ice thousands upon thousands of feet thick. Geologists have found traces of much earlier ice ages on other continents, but none seems to match this one in extent.

It was in these dramatic and stressful times that our own species, humankind, finally made its appearance on the stage of life. In a few thousand years we seem to have dominated the whole planet and modified it to our own uses. But as we go about our daily lives, we rarely pause to consider that the Ice Age may not be over. The experts tell us there have been balmy intervals between the glacial advances before. While some experts suggest we have good reason to worry about the dangers of global warming in the next few decades, it may be that our more distant descendants will see the great cold return yet again.

A SURVEY OF THE MINERALS

Next, some of the basic facts and concepts of *mineralogy*, one of the oldest branches of geology. As you can tell from its name, it is the study of *minerals*. But what is a mineral, exactly?

Actually, it's not easy to define. Scientists say that a substance is a mineral if it is "naturally occurring"— that is, if it isn't created artificially, in a laboratory for instance. Further, it can't be made up of organic substances that are the building blocks of living tissue. Still, a mineral does have some sort of orderly internal structure.

However elusive their precise description is, minerals have an immense significance to most geologists. After all, they are the primary building blocks of all rocks. In fact, a rock can be thought of as an aggregate of one or more minerals.

1. The Crystal Systems • In most minerals, the orderly internal structure mentioned earlier is found in the form of *crystals*. Crystals are distinguished by certain characteristic shapes, formed by their flat sides, or *faces*. You can probably think of some crystals you've seen. The tiny grains in your dinnertable salt shaker are actually simple, square-faced crystals. Snowflakes are crystals, too, though they are much more complex than those of salt.

Mineralogists classify crystals into six overall groups, or *systems* (see Figure 3-7). As the illustration shows, the different crystal systems are defined by imaginary lines, called *axes* (the plural of *axis*). Each axis runs from the center of one crystal face, straight to the center of the face opposite it. Crystals have a total of either three or four axes. It is the lengths of the axes, as well as how they meet each other in the center of a crystal, that determine which crystal system is which.

The simplest crystal system is called the *isometric*. Here the three axes are all the same length, and all meet at right angles (90 degrees). This arrangement means the crystals are cube-shaped. If this makes you think of the square-faced salt grains, there's a good reason. Salt crystals are one of the most well-known members of the isometric system.

Next comes the *tetragonal* system. It too has three axes that all meet at right angles, but one axis is a different length than the other two. Zircon, a common mineral often found in granite and other rocks, is one example of a substance with a tetragonal crystal structure.

There is only one system that has four axes. It is

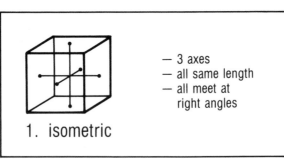

1. isometric

— 3 axes
— all same length
— all meet at
   right angles

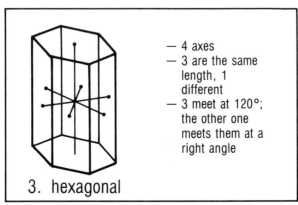

2. tetragonal

— 3 axes
— 2 are the same
  length, 1
  different
— all meet at
   right angles

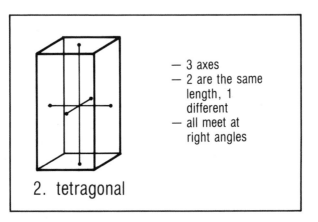

3. hexagonal

— 4 axes
— 3 are the same
  length, 1
  different
— 3 meet at 120°;
   the other one
   meets them at a
   right angle

Figure 3-7. *The six crystal systems*

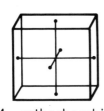

— 3 axes
— all different
  lengths
— all meet at
  right angles

4. orthorhombic

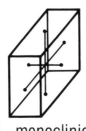

— 3 axes
— all different
  lengths
— 2 meet at
  right angles;
  the other meets
  them at angles
  that are *not* 90°

5. monoclinic

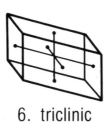

— 3 axes
— all different
  lengths
— all meet at angles
  that are *not* 90°

6. triclinic

the *hexagonal*. All but one of the axes are the same length—these intersect each other at wide, 120-degree angles. The remaining axis is not only longer or shorter than the others—it also meets them at a right angle. One of the best-known of all minerals, quartz, forms the six-sided crystals typical of the hexagonal system.

Now things get a bit more complex. The three axes of the *orthorhombic* system are all different lengths. However, they all meet at right angles. One highly prized orthorhombic mineral is topaz, a glassy gemstone that occurs in various colors.

Another important type of mineral, mica, is an example of the *monoclinic* system. Its crystals have three axes with no two the same length; two meet at a right angle, but the other must intersect at an angle that is not 90 degrees.

The last of the six crystal systems is the *triclinic*. The three axes are all of unequal lengths, and all meet at angles that are not 90 degrees. Microcline is one mineral that forms triclinic crystals.

Since the molecules of each kind of mineral usually arrange themselves into just one of these crystal systems, you can often use a mineral's crystal shape to help identify it. Here's one example. Sometimes two different minerals, quartz and fluorite, resemble each other in color and overall appearance. But while fluorite forms cube-shape isometric crystals, quartz has six-sided, prismlike crystals of the hexagonal system. So samples of these two substances can be distinguished.

2. The Mohs Hardness Scale • Another way to distinguish similar-looking minerals is by their relative hardness. Mineralogists use what is known as the Mohs Hardness Scale, with ratings from 1 (the softest minerals) to 10 (the hardest). It is based on how easily substances can be scratched. The mineral gypsum is rated at 2 because it is very soft. Orthoclase, at 6, easily scratches it; and superhard diamond, at 10, in turn scratches orthoclase and any other mineral with a number lower than its own.

The complete Mohs Hardness Scale is shown in Figure 3-8. You can figure out the rating of an unknown mineral by scratching it against known mineral specimens, or in some cases against your fingernail or common metal objects. For instance, if you have a mystery mineral sample that scratches quartz, it's harder than 7. If it can be scratched by corundum, it's softer than 9. Since it falls between 7 and 9, it must be 8. In the same way, if your sample can be scratched by a pocket knife blade (a hardness of 5), but not by a copper penny (a hardness of 3), it's at 4 on the scale. Figure 3-9 depicts representative minerals on Mohs Hardness Scale.

3. The Streak Plate Test • Another method of identifying minerals involves the use of a piece of white por-

RATING	TYPICAL MINERAL	CAN ALSO BE SCRATCHED BY:
1 (softest)	talc	
2	gypsum	fingernail
3	calcite	copper coin
4	fluorite	
5	apatite	pocket knife
6	orthoclase	steel file
7	quartz	
8	topaz	
9	corundum	
10 (hardest)	diamond	

Figure 3-8. *The Mohs Hardness Scale*

Figure 3–9. The minerals of Mohs Hardness scale:
talc, gypsum, calcite, fluorite, apatite, orthoclase,
quartz, topaz, corundum, diamond

orthoclase

quartz

topaz

corundum

diamond

celain known as a streak plate. Some minerals, when rubbed against the plate, produce a telltale color. One good example of this is the bright scarlet streak produced by a mercury ore, cinnabar. Don't be disappointed, though, if the streak test doesn't help all the time. The identity of quite a few substances must be pinned down by other means.

4. The Chemical Groups • Minerals are also frequently classified by their chemical makeup. The first and simplest category is the *native elements*—minerals made up of a single kind of atom. *Sulfur* is one good example of a native element; others include some of the most coveted substances on earth: *gold, silver, copper,* and the most precious form of carbon, *diamond. Graphite,* another native element, is carbon, too, in a humbler but still important form.

The next group, the *sulfides,* are compounds with at least two kinds of atoms—one of which is always sulfur. The sulfides include several economically important minerals, including *cinnabar,* the copper ores *chalcocite* and *chalcopyrite,* the lead ore *galena,* and *pyrite,* also known as "fool's gold" because of its slight resemblance to everybody's favorite yellow metal.

The *oxides,* consisting of oxygen combined with metal atoms, contain important ores, too: *bauxite* for aluminum, *cuprite* for copper, *magnetite* and *hematite* for iron. As its name suggests, magnetite has an additional claim to fame—it is strongly magnetic and will attract iron filings, sewing needles, and other susceptible metal objects.

One other oxide is worth special note. Corundum, already familiar to us from its place on the Mohs Hardness Scale, occurs in various colors. Its blue form is *sapphire,* while its dark red version is *ruby.* So two of the world's most beautiful and sought-after gemstones come from one mineral!

The *halides* is a smaller group. It consists of compounds that include the elements chlorine, boron, fluorine, or iodine. Two of the more common halides belong to the cube-forming isometric crystal system: *halite,* better known as *rock salt,* and *fluorite.*

Two common rock-forming minerals, *calcite* and *dolomite,* are carbon compounds of the *carbonates* group. Other carbonates include two beautiful copper ores, the light blue *azurite* and the bright green *malachite.*

The mineral *borax* is the best-known member of the small *borates* group. Its uses are many, from soap to medicines to an ingredient for rocket fuel. On the other hand, *soda niter,* mined for fertilizers and explosives, is one of the *nitrates.* As you might guess, borates are compounds containing the element boron, and nitrates are based on nitrogen.

The *phosphates* group has a bigger roster of minerals. Among these are the hexagonal *apatite* and the sky-blue gemstone *turquoise* that is used so skillfully by the native jewelry makers of the American Southwest.

The *sulfates* take their name from a molecule they all contain, which is made up of one sulfur atom and four oxygen atoms. Two common sulfates are *gypsum,* used in plaster and soil conditioners, and *barite,* a primary source of the element barium.

Our last group, the *silicates,* is the biggest of all, making up about one quarter of all the minerals. The element silicon is the common link in all silicates. Some of the most important and frequently encountered members of this large group are *quartz, olivine, hornblende, talc,* and such *feldspars* as *orthoclase* and *microcline.* Also included are *mica* minerals, such as the dark-hued *biotite* and the transparent *muscovite.* Gemstones, too, are represented by *tourmaline, topaz, beryl,* and *garnet.*

5. A Mineral Identification Table • The table shown in Figure 3-10 lists the minerals described in the preceding section and gives you their "personality traits" lined

NAME	CHEMICAL GRP.	CRYSTAL SYS.	COLOR	HARDNESS	STREAK
Apatite	Phosphates	Hexagonal	Green or Brown	5–5.5	None
Azurite	Carbonates	Monoclinic	Azure Blue	3.5–4	None
Barite	Sulfates	Orthorhombic	Various	3–3.5	None
Bauxite	Oxides	Various	Various	1–3	None
Beryl	Silicates	Hexagonal	Various	7.5–8	None
Biotite	Silicates	Monoclinic	Black or Brown	2.5–3	None
(a Mica)					
Borax	Borates	Monoclinic	Clear or White	2–2.5	None
Calcite	Carbonates	Hexagonal	Clear or White	2.5–3	None
Chalcocite	Sulfides	Orthorhombic	Gray to Black	2.5–3	Gray–black
Chalcopyrite	Sulfides	Tetragonal	Brass–yellow	3.5–4	Green–black
Cinnabar	Sulfides	Hexagonal	Red to Brown	2.5	Scarlet
Copper	Native Elem.	Isometric	Copper–red	2.5–3	None
Corundum	Oxides	Hexagonal	Various	9	None
Cuprite	Oxides	Isometric	Red	3.5–4	Red–brown
Diamond	Native Elem.	Isometric	Clear	10	None
(a form of Carbon)					
Dolomite	Carbonates	Hexagonal	Pink	3.5–4	None
Fluorite	Halides	Isometric	Various	4	None
Galena	Sulfides	Isometric	Lead–gray	2.5	Lead–gray
Garnet	Silicates	Isometric	Various	6.5–7.5	White
Gold	Native Elem.	Isometric	Yellow	2.5–3	None

Mineral	Composition	Crystal System	Color	Hardness	Streak
Graphite (a form of Carbon)	Native Elem.	Hexagonal	Black	1-2	Black
Gypsum	Sulfates	Monoclinic	White or Clear	2	None
Halite	Halides	Isometric	Clear or White	2.5	None
Hematite	Oxides	Hexagonal	Brown to Black	5.5-6.5	Red
Hornblende	Silicates	Monoclinic	Black	5-6	None
Magnetite	Oxides	Isometric	Iron-black	6	Black
Malachite	Carbonates	Monoclinic	Bright Green	3.5-4	Light Green
Microcline (a Feldspar)	Silicates	Triclinic	White to Yellow	6	None
Muscovite (a Mica)	Silicates	Monoclinic	Clear	2-2.5	None
Olivine	Silicates	Orthorhombic	Olive Green	6.5-7	None
Orthoclase (a Feldspar)	Silicates	Monoclinic	White or Gray	6	White
Pyrite	Sulfides	Isometric	Brass-yellow	6-6.5	Green-black
Quartz	Silicates	Hexagonal	Various	7	None
Silver	Native Elem.	Isometric	Silver-white	2.5-3	Silver-white
Soda Niter	Nitrates	Hexagonal	White	2	None
Sulfur	Native Elem.	Orthorhombic	Yellow	1.5-2.5	None
Talc	Silicates	Monoclinic	Various	1	None
Topaz	Silicates	Orthorhombic	Various	8	None
Tourmaline	Silicates	Hexagonal	Various	7-7.5	None
Turquoise	Phosphates	Triclinic	Blue-green	6	None

Figure 3-10. A mineral identification table

up, so you can see them all at a glance. To identify an unknown mineral sample, first match one of its characteristics, for example its color, with the minerals in the table that fit it. Then go on to a second characteristic, such as hardness, and so on, till all but one most likely mineral has been eliminated.

COMMON ROCK TYPES

Of course, minerals by themselves are not the whole story, since they usually combine to form masses of rock. It is these larger structures that determine the way our planet's crust looks and behaves. Most people consider rocks to be just pieces of stone, and leave it at that. And that isn't a bad everyday definition of them. But geologists use the fact that rocks are assemblages of one or more minerals to unravel mysteries about how earlier versions of the earth came to be. Sometimes a single rock, when interpreted by a knowledgeable person, can tell a remarkable story of an ancient environment that existed hundreds of millions of years ago.

Lithology is the branch of geology concerned with the study of rock types. Lithologists recognize three overall categories of rocks: *igneous, sedimentary,* and *metamorphic.* Let's take a look at each, and see which rock types are characteristic of them.

1. Igneous Rocks • This group comes into being when molten rock, known as *magma,* cools into the solid state (Figure 3-11). When magma solidifies underground, the result is *intrusive* rock. Two common forms of intrusive igneous rocks are *granite* and *gabbro.* Granite is rich in the compound silica and contains quartz, feldspars, and other minerals. It is usually light-colored and made up of well-defined crystals of varying sizes. Gabbro, on the other hand, is a dark rock, rich in iron and magnesium. It too has crystals that are easily seen by the naked eye.

basalt

rhyolite

Figure 3–11. *Igneous rock types: granite, gabbro, basalt, rhyolite*

Magma in the form of *lava* sometimes does make it all the way to the earth's surface, through volcanic vents or fissures. As the lava cools it becomes *extrusive* rock. One important example of this type is *rhyolite*, which is the extrusive equivalent of granite. You probably won't confuse the two, though, since rhyolite is finely textured, with smaller individual crystals that are hard or impossible to distinguish from one another without a microscope.

Another very widespread type of extrusive rock is named *basalt* or *traprock*. It is the chemical equivalent of gabbro, though its texture is much finer. Not only is it found outcropping on many continents; it is also the material that makes up the vast expanses of the earth's seafloor as well as our moon's younger rock formations. (These "younger" lunar rocks are 3 to 4 billion years old!) Basalt is usually black, dark brown, or reddish brown, and often it is pitted with holes left by gas bubbles.

2. Sedimentary Rocks • This group seems to have a more peaceful origin, since it is produced by the gradual accumulation of particles called *sediments*—tiny crystals, mud, sand, stones, or the remains of animals and other creatures—instead of being formed from magma (Figure 3-12). Regardless of their exact composition, however, sedimentary rocks have one trait in common; they are formed into layers called *strata* (a single layer is called a *stratum*). One particular stratum may be only an inch or two thick, while another may extend many feet from top to bottom.

The sedimentary rocks with the largest sediment sizes are *conglomerate* and *breccia* (pronounced "bresh-ee-uh"). These have particles larger—often *much* larger—than 2 millimeters (about 1/12 inch). Conglomerates are made up of rounded particles, such as pebbles or cobbles, while breccias contain more pointed, angular fragments. Brec-

Figure 3–12. Sedimentary rock types: sandstone, shale (with plant fossils), shell limestone

Figure 3–13. Metamorphic rock types: gneiss, schist, slate, marble

cias often form quite close to where their large pieces were first broken free by erosion. In a similar way, conglomerate sediments are too large to travel very long distances from their point of origin. They tend to form where powerful, rushing water begins to slow down—for example, when a fast-flowing mountain stream enters a larger and more stately river.

As we descend in sediment size we next find *sandstone*, with particles ranging from 2 millimeters down to 1/16 millimeter. Sandstone is formed in a number of different ways. In common with conglomerate, it may indicate part of an ancient riverbed; or it may be part of sediments that were deposited offshore, fairly close to a seacoast. In the states of Utah and Arizona it is even possible to find huge, breathtaking sandstone beds that document desert sand dunes of the Mesozoic Era.

Finer yet in particle size is *shale*, a rock made from sediments less than 1/16 millimeter. If you tried the second Amateur Geologist Exploration in Chapter One, you already know that the smallest and lightest sediments suspended in water are the last to settle to the bottom. So it's not surprising that shale forms primarily in quiet-water environments such as the great coal swamps of the Pennsylvania period, or in the stiller waters a good distance off a coastline. Incidentally, shale's smooth texture makes it one of the best fossil-bearing rocks.

There is one other basic kind of sedimentary rock: *limestone*. Its origin is different from the others since it comes from the accumulation of remains of living things, or from a process known as chemical precipitation. Some types of limestone consist of tiny fragments of shells and other animal parts; others, which are the result of the precipitation process, are primarily deposits of the mineral calcite. A close relative of limestone, *dolostone*, takes its name from dolomite, the most important mineral it contains. Generally speaking, limestone and dolostone form still farther offshore, beyond even the shale zone.

3. Metamorphic Rocks • The earth's crust is an often unstable place. In the long course of our planet's history countless igneous and sedimentary rock formations have been pushed, stretched, squeezed, and warped as continents have collided and new mountain ranges have been born. These formations, which have been altered by tremendous forces without totally melting, are changed, or *metamorphosed,* into rocks with characteristics all their own (Figure 3-13).

If you're in an area of metamorphic rock, one variety you're likely to see is *gneiss* (pronounced "nice"). Sometimes it resembles granite a great deal—as it should, since gneiss is often metamorphosed granite, or something very similar. But gneiss can be distinguished from its parent rock by the way its crystals are lined up in distinct light and dark bands. When crystals line up this way in metamorphic rocks, geologists refer to it as *foliation.* *Schist* is another rock variety with foliation. Though it doesn't have light and dark bands, careful examination reveals its somewhat layered look.

One of the hardest of all rocks is *quartzite.* It is metamorphosed sandstone, and as its name implies it is composed of tough, resistant quartz. On the other hand, when shale is metamorphosed it becomes *slate.* (One way to distinguish these two rocks is to listen to them. When struck with a hammer, metamorphic slate usually makes a sharp clinking sound, while sedimentary shale produces a duller sound.) The metamorphic rock *marble* resembles its sedimentary source, limestone, too. Marble can usually be distinguished by its especially smooth, sugary texture and its shiny surfaces.

A LOOK AT FOSSILS

If you're a fossil collector already, you probably know that the chances of your finding a complete dinosaur or woolly mammoth skeleton aren't particularly good—un-

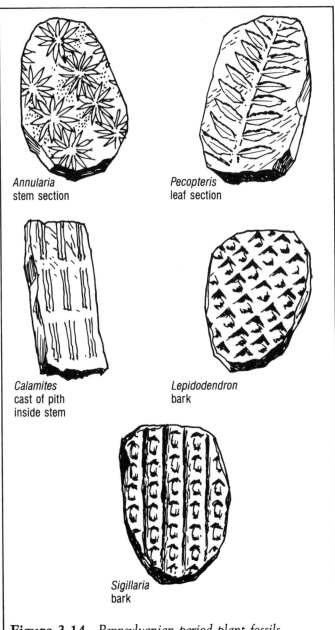

Annularia
stem section

Pecopteris
leaf section

Calamites
cast of pith
inside stem

Lepidodendron
bark

Sigillaria
bark

Figure 3-14. *Pennsylvanian period plant fossils*

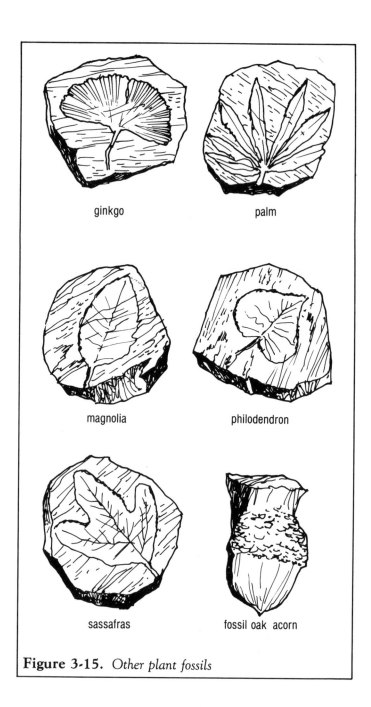

ginkgo

palm

magnolia

philodendron

sassafras

fossil oak acorn

Figure 3-15. *Other plant fossils*

less you go to a museum or join a professional expedition headed by a *paleontologist* (a person who studies ancient life as it's revealed in the fossil record). The fossils you're most likely to find are the less dramatic, but just as intriguing, remains of either plants or the kind of animals known as *invertebrates*—that is, the creatures that lack backbones common to mammals, reptiles, birds, amphibians, and fish. Many invertebrates live in the ocean, but some, such as insects, spiders, and terrestrial snails, have adapted superbly to life in the open air. Before we consider them further, though, let's turn to fossils from the great and remarkable Kingdom of Plants.

1. Plant Fossils • The earliest land plants in the fossil record appeared long ago, in the Silurian period. But the most prevalent plant fossils found today date from the Pennsylvanian period, the time of the great swamps that covered much of the eastern half of the United States. In some areas of Illinois and Indiana, for instance, coal-bearing sedimentary strata of Pennsylvanian age may be found. These rock formations often contain round or oblong lumps of rock known as *concretions* and *coal balls*. When a concretion is carefully cracked open with a rock hammer it may reveal a beautifully detailed section of an ancient leaf, or even part of a stem or bark from a long-extinct tree species.

The illustrations in Figure 3-14 show a small selection of plant fossils found in coal ball beds. The *Annularia* and *Calamites* specimens represent ancestors of our modern horsetails and scouring rushes. *Pecopteris* was one of the seed ferns, trees that were very successful in their own day, but are now totally extinct. Both *Lepidodendron* and *Sigillaria* were trees, too, though their only surviving descendants are the humble club mosses found growing on the floor of forests in New England and other parts of North America.

It is also possible to find the remains of more recent

and more familiar plants that date from the end of the Mesozoic era up to the present times. Leaves from magnolias, fig trees, laurels, sycamores, and sassafras (see Figure 3-15) are among those found well preserved in sedimentary rocks and even sometimes in volcanic ash.

2. Corals • These underwater creatures may seem very plantlike, but actually they are invertebrate animals that form strange, complicated structures. Two kinds of fossil corals prevalent in the Paleozoic era were the *tabulate* and *rugose* types. Tabulate corals were arranged in groups of many small chambers, such as those of *Favosites*, while rugose corals such as *Streptelasma* were cone- or horn-shaped (Figure 3-16).

3. Brachiopods • Among the most common and important invertebrate fossils are those of the brachiopods (Figure 3-17). At first glance these sea creatures seem to be clams. They have the same basic shape, and they have two shells, called *valves*, that protect the soft-fleshed

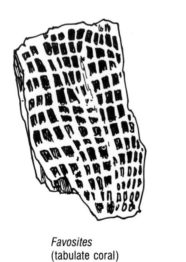

Favosites
(tabulate coral)

Streptelasma
(rugose coral)

Figure 3-16. *Fossil corals*

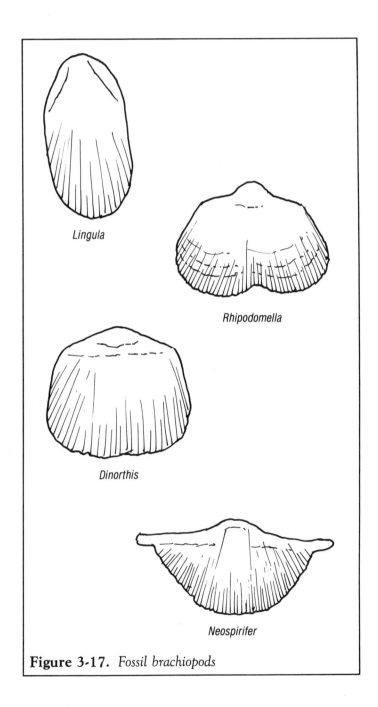

Lingula

Rhipodomella

Dinorthis

Neospirifer

Figure 3-17. *Fossil brachiopods*

animal inside. But brachiopods evolved quite separately from clams. One telltale sign of this can be found in their outward appearance. Unlike clam valves, the two valves of a brachiopod usually differ noticeably from one another in shape and size.

One humble brachiopod, named *Lingula,* has set an astonishing survival record. Its kind has remained unchanged for millions upon millions of generations, from the Ordovician period in the early Paleozoic, through all of the Mesozoic and Cenozoic! Most other species of plants and animals have much less time on earth before they become extinct. The fact that such brachiopods as *Rhipodomella, Dinorthis,* and *Neospirifer* flourished for shorter timespans helps geologists to date rock formations accurately. If they find *Neospirifer* in one rock layer, for instance, they know the stratum must be of Permian age.

4. Mollusks • This dominant group of invertebrates contains many familiar marine and terrestrial creatures, both in the fossil record and thriving in our own time. In fact, the mollusks are so numerous and diverse that it's best to consider their three main sections, one at a time.

The first of these is the *gastropods* (Figure 3-18), the snails and slugs. Ancient snail shells, including *Bellerophon, Maclurites, Worthenia,* and *Murchisonia,* can be abundant in fossil-bearing sedimentary rock. As with the brachiopods described earlier, some extinct snail species make very good *index fossils*—that is, they are restricted to just one relatively short time period, and so indicate the exact age of the beds they're in.

The next type of mollusk is the *cephalopods,* represented in modern times by the squid, the octopus, and the beautiful chambered nautilus. Their extinct forms frequently lived in straight, coiled, or partly coiled shells that are usually much bigger than snail shells. Some

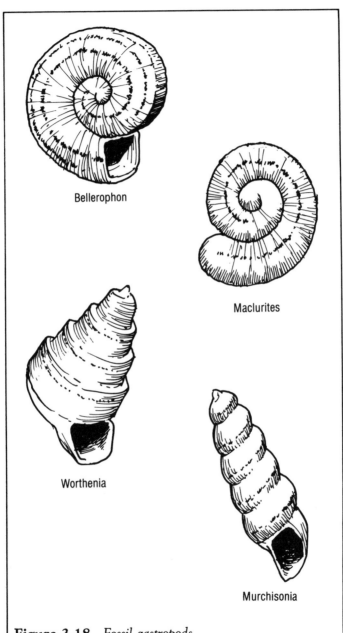

Bellerophon

Maclurites

Worthenia

Murchisonia

Figure 3-18. *Fossil gastropods*

Mesozoic cephalopods, for instance, lived in spiral-shaped shells as big as tractor tires!

The cephalopods known as *ammonites* make particularly good Mesozoic index fossils. These marine contemporaries of the dinosaurs sported wavy patterns on their shells that are called *sutures*. Each species had its own distinctive kind of sutures, making especially precise identification and age determination possible. In Figure 3-19 *Stephanoceras* and *Spiroceras* are examples of ammonites, while *Aturia* and *Belemnites* exemplify other types of cephalopods.

The third section of mollusks, the *pelecypods*, are better known to us as oysters, clams, and their relatives. Although they are travelers along a much different evolutionary path, they do seem to resemble brachiopods at first, until you notice that clams and the other pelecypods have two valves or shells that are almost identical to one another. As we have learned, pairs of brachiopod valves are generally uneven in shape or size.

Nowadays pelecypods are much more common in seas and lakes than brachiopods are, but the geologic record indicates that their success story stretches far back into the Paleozoic Era. Among the many common fossil types are *Ostrea, Exogyra, Mytilus,* and the well-known scallop shells of *Pecten* (Figure 3-20).

5. Arthropods • This, too, is a major invertebrate group which contains some very well-known animals: insects, spiders, centipedes, and such crustaceans as crabs, shrimps, and lobsters. These creatures can be found in the fossil record at various points, but other types of arthropods are at least as important to the paleontologist.

Among these, the extinct *trilobites* are some of the most common arthropods in Paleozoic rocks. The many different species of trilobites vary greatly in shape and size, but they conform to a basic plan of a head shield

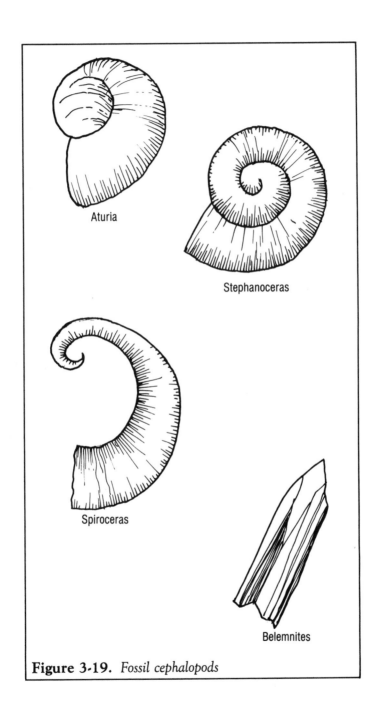

Aturia

Stephanoceras

Spiroceras

Belemnites

Figure 3-19. *Fossil cephalopods*

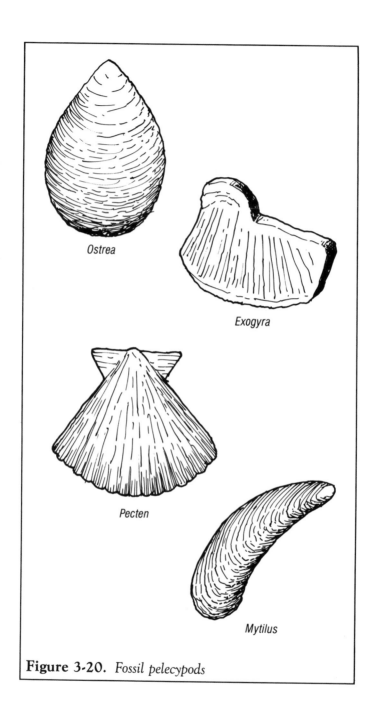

Ostrea

Exogyra

Pecten

Mytilus

Figure 3-20. *Fossil pelecypods*

or *cephalon*, a middle section called the *thorax*, and the *pygidium*, or tailpiece. Often these individual sections are preserved separately. Three frequently found trilobites are *Eodiscus*, *Paradoxides*, and *Olenellus* (Figure 3-21).

One other type of arthropod deserves special mention, though it is by no means as common as trilobites. The odd-looking but impressive *eurypterids*, or sea scorpions, held sway primarily in the Silurian and Devonian Periods. *Eurypterus* is a good example of these strange creatures, some of which grew to be as large as a small pickup truck.

6. Echinoderms • This group of invertebrates includes such modern marine animals as starfish and sea urchins. One of the most important echinoderm fossils can easily be mistaken for a plant. Its adult form has what seems to be a flower head, as well as a long stem that anchors it to the ocean floor. This is the *crinoid*, or sea lily. Shown below in Figure 3-22 are the crowns or uppermost parts of two types of crinoids, *Taxacrinus* and *Isocrinus*. Often the stems are the only parts that are found; when their segments break off, they resemble circular or star-shaped buttons.

7. Graptolites • Of all the animal remains from the early Paleozoic Era, graptolites are some of the very best index fossils. They are normally encountered as flat carbon films in black shales. Like crinoids, they can be mistaken for plants, since they consist of branchlike structures that, on closer inspection, hold tiny tubes or cups. One kind of graptolite is pictured in Figure 3-22.

8. Vertebrate Fossils • As noted before, your chances of finding a complete skeleton of a large extinct animal aren't terrific, but that doesn't mean you won't come

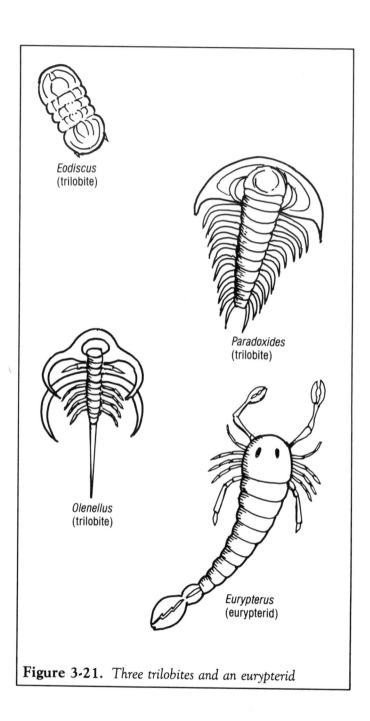

Figure 3-21. *Three trilobites and an eurypterid*

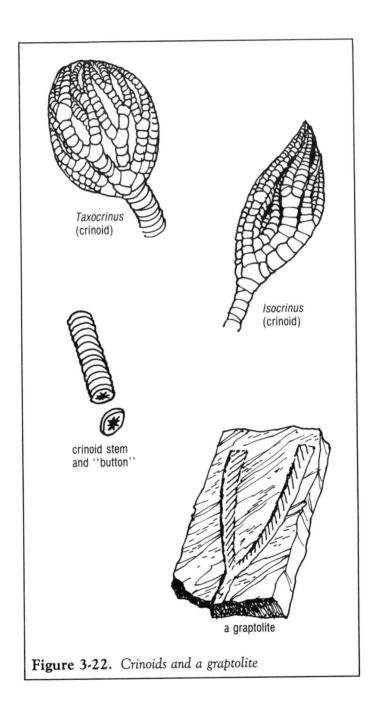

Taxocrinus
(crinoid)

Isocrinus
(crinoid)

crinoid stem
and ''button''

a graptolite

Figure 3-22. *Crinoids and a graptolite*

across less spectacular vertebrate remains. Fossil shark's teeth are quite common in marine sediments, and if you're out West, you may even come across one of the famous Green River fish preserved in volcanic ash from eruptions in the Tertiary Period. Dinosaur tracks can be found in various locations, including the Connecticut River Valley of southern New England. Remember, though, that you should never go fossil-hunting for these, especially on public land, unless local regulations allow you to.

Chapter 4

Projects for the Amateur Geologist

THE WORLD OF MINERALS

In this final chapter we look at some geology activities you can try for school projects, for a science fair, or for your own enjoyment. As you'll see, there are six kinds of activities in each section. While they can be done just as they're described here, don't hesitate to combine or modify them to suit your interests.

Collecting and Classifying:
Mineral Hunting

Information
Needed:

☐ The location of one or more good mineral collecting sites (the AAPG *Geological Highway Map* for your region lists many of these sites)

☐ The Mineral Identification Table (Figure 3-10)

☐ A field guide to minerals

☐ A boxed mineral set (optional)

Field
Equipment:

☐ A rock hammer

☐ Safety glasses or other protective eyewear

☐ At least one sample collecting bag

☐ A field notebook

☐ A marking pen

Other Supplies:	☐ A display box, tray, or shelf for your own mineral collection
	☐ Sample labels
	☐ 3 by 5 cards
	☐ A 3 by 5 card file box
	☐ White enamel model paint
	☐ Red enamel model paint
	☐ A model paintbrush and a sewing needle

The purpose of this project is to collect as many mineral specimens as you can, identify them, and then classify them by their crystal systems and chemical families.

Once you've identified a good mineral-collecting location, get permission to hunt there by contacting the owner (on private land) or the local authorities (for public lands such as parks and state forests). Some of the best-known collecting areas cannot be visited unless you pay an entrance fee, so check before you go. If permission is granted, take along your rock hammer and collection bag—and good luck!

Remember that mineral-hunting, like fossil-hunting, is a matter of patience. You may spend hours looking in outcrops or rock piles without finding a single good specimen. On the other hand, you may find several interesting samples in just a few minutes. Whenever possible, choose specimens with good crystal faces, and those which can be easily removed or distinguished from the rocks that contain them. Take careful field notes, since they will form the basis of the information file you'll compile later.

If you visit more than one collecting site on a particular day, make sure you keep samples from each location separate and label them as you collect them. In addition, always be careful that the minerals you gather do not rub against or scratch each other in the sample bag. Some may be easily damaged or broken.

The next step takes place indoors, when you identify and label the specimens you've collected. Even before you determine the exact identity of your minerals, you should review your field notes while your memory is fresh. That way you won't forget which samples came from each location you visited.

When you are ready to do the detective work, take your field guide to minerals, and a boxed mineral set if you have one, and match your own samples as best you can with the examples given. You may wish to turn back to the description of the different crystal shapes in Chapter Three.

When you have collected and identified several specimens, refer to the Mineral Identification Table. Among other things it lists each mineral's chemical group and crystal system. Using this information, you can arrange your collection according to one of these categories. For instance, if you want to display your specimens by chemical group, you can show the oxides on one shelf or tray, the silicates on another, and so on. The same thing goes for crystal systems: you can sort your samples into groups that display the characteristics of a particular crystal form.

One key ingredient to any good collection is proper labeling and documentation. The first step is to number your samples. Make a small solid circle with the white model paint on one side of each specimen; let it dry thoroughly. Then put the specimen's number on the white circle, using the red paint and a very fine brush or the tip of a sewing needle. The illustration in Figure 4-1 demonstrates how this should look.

Since you'll probably want to display your collection at some point, at home or at a science fair, you should make small tags that identify your samples for other people. Figure 4-2 shows one kind of label that can be placed next to the sample it describes.

For your own records, however, you'll want to have

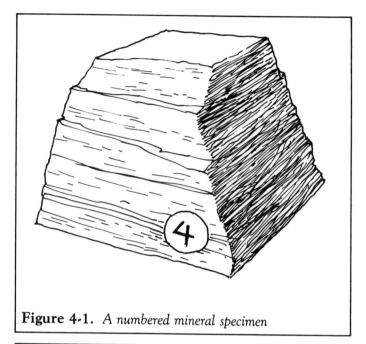

Figure 4-1. *A numbered mineral specimen*

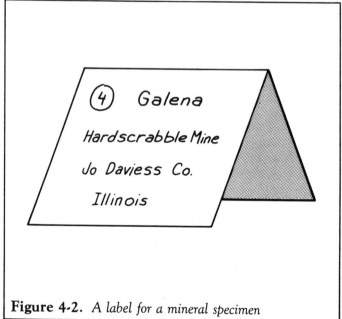

Figure 4-2. *A label for a mineral specimen*

more documentation than you can put on a small label. For this, you can use one 3 by 5 card for each sample. Figure 4-3 is an example of the kind of information to include on the card.

Keep the completed sample cards in numerical order in the file box, where you can refer to them easily.

Chances are that you will find some specimens that you can't identify immediately. Don't throw them out—it's very likely that you'll learn what they are later on. So fill out as much information about them as you can, and be patient.

---

mineral specimen no. 4

collection site: hardscrabble mine, Jo Daviess County, Illinois
collection date: 22 June 1991
name of mineral: galena
crystal system: isometric
chemical group: sulfides
other information: galena is an important lead ore

Figure 4-3. *A specimen card from a mineral collection file*

The *scientific method* of experimenting is based on a simple but effective procedure: The experimenter first makes a *hypothesis*, or a beginning hunch about something, and then verifies whether that hunch is right. In this sec-

Experimenting:
Verifying the Identity of Mineral Specimens

Information Needed:	☐ The Mineral Identification Table (Figure 3-10)
	☐ The Mohs Hardness Scale (Figure 3-8)
	☐ A field guide to minerals
Equipment:	☐ A streak plate
	☐ A copper coin (a penny will do nicely)
	☐ A pocket knife
	☐ A steel file
	☐ A spare piece of clean quartz

tion you'll do just that. You'll test your first hunches about your mineral specimens, and see whether they still seem correct after you have investigated them more thoroughly.

In the previous section you identified your mineral samples by matching them with a field guide to minerals, or with minerals in a boxed set. But it's always best to check the identification at least one or two other ways—that's what the verification process is all about. In this case, you will do a simple experiment by checking each of your samples for streak color and hardness.

Start with the first sample. Take your streak plate and rub an edge of the specimen firmly but carefully along it (in this and the hardness test, be careful to use the least attractive part of the sample, so you won't damage its appearance). Did the sample leave a streak? If so, what was its color? Record the results.

Next, determine the sample's hardness. Try to scratch it, carefully, with the piece of quartz. If it *cannot* be scratched by quartz, but instead scratches it, it has a hardness rating of 8 or higher, as the Mohs Hardness Scale shows. But if the quartz does scratch your sample, it has a hardness rating of 7 or less, and you'll have to keep trying. Does the steel file scratch it? If so, the specimen has a hardness of 6 or less. Then try the pocket knife and, if necessary, the copper coin and your fingernail, till you've reached the point where it can no longer be scratched. That point is its hardness rating. Record the sample's hardness number next to its streak test results.

Now refer to the Mineral Identification Table. Look at the listing for the mineral you think your sample may be. Do the hardness rating and streak color that are listed there match your own results? If they do, congratulations! You have additional evidence that your original guess was right. If they don't, however, there's no reason to give up. Go back to the field guide and look for other minerals that are likely candidates. They, too, can be checked with their hardness ratings and streak colors in the Mineral Identification Table, and in most cases you'll be able to pin down the correct identity through the process of elimination.

Illustrating a Method of Mineral Identification: The Mohs Hardness Scale

Information Needed:	☐ The Mohs Hardness Scale (Figure 3-8)
Equipment:	☐ Posterboard or stout cardboard, for a poster
	☐ Small samples of minerals listed on the Mohs Hardness Scale.
	☐ Photographs or drawings of rare and unobtainable minerals listed on the Mohs Hardness Scale (for example, diamond and topaz)
	☐ Glue for mounting mineral samples, photographs, and drawings on a poster
	☐ Marker pens of various colors

This project is relatively simple, but it's ideal for science fairs because it demonstrates a classic method of mineral identification in an eye-catching way.

First assemble samples or pictures of all the mineral types listed on the Mohs Hardness Scale. Then neatly print the scale in large block letters on a poster board that is roughly 36 inches tall by 24 inches wide. Use markers of different colors to add to the poster's visual appeal.

When you've printed the hardness scale, carefully glue the mineral specimens and pictures next to their names.

On the other hand, you may be able to come up with another format or style that works better for you. Be creative!

Highlighting Your Local Mineralogy: Assembling an Assortment of Minerals from Your Own State

Information Needed:	☐ The Mineral Identification Table (Figure 3-10)
	☐ The AAPG Geological Highway Map of the region that includes your state (optional)
Equipment:	☐ A collection of mineral specimens found in your state
	☐ Posterboard or stout cardboard, for two posters
	☐ A map of your state (a roadmap is fine)
	☐ Colored stick pins
	☐ Rubber cement or glue for paper
	☐ Glue or cement to attach small mineral specimens to a poster

You may live in a state where the mineral resources play an important role in the region's past or present economy. But even if you don't, you'll find that a display of your own state's characteristic mineral deposits attracts the interest of many people.

Begin by cementing your mineral specimens to one of the two posters. Neatly label each specimen by giving its name, its economic significance (if any), and the part of the state where it is found (Figure 4-4).

Next, carefully mount your state map on the other poster, using rubber cement or another suitable glue. You can use the colored pins to indicate where your own mineral specimens were found, or you can use them to point out important mineral deposits in general. One way to learn more about these locations is to check the AAPG Geological Highway Map for your area, since it lists famous mineral collecting and mining localities.

The two posters, displayed together, make an attractive and informative exhibit for your home, for a display area at your school, and especially for science fairs.

Explaining the Basic Forms of Minerals: Crystal System Models

Information Needed:	☐ The illustrations of crystal systems shown in Figure 3-7
Equipment:	☐ Long match sticks, pipe cleaners, or straight drinking straws
	☐ Glue or some other means of attaching match sticks or straws to one another (not needed if you use pipe cleaners instead)
	☐ Spray paint (optional)
	☐ A small bottle of model paint (optional)
	☐ A model paintbrush (optional)
	☐ 3 by 5 cards
	☐ A small T-square, a protractor, or another suitable device for measuring right angles

minerals of Arizona

 native copper – many economic uses—found in spoil pile in Bisbee

 gypsum – used in plaster— found in rock strata along the Beeline, in the Four Peaks area between Fort McDowell and Payson

 malachite - copper ore— found in spoil pile in Superior

 selenite – a form of gypsum— found on the floor of the Sonoran Desert, Maricopa County

Figure 4-4. *Display samples of your finds in a "minerals of your state" poster.*

If you are a good model builder or are adept at constructing things in general, this project should appeal to you. The purpose is to build three-dimensional models of the six crystal systems shown in Figure 3-7. Using the illustrations and specifications there as a guide, consider your match sticks, straws, or pipe cleaners to be the sides and axes of the models and connect them. Make sure the models are rigid and securely fastened. For example, your model for the *isometric* system would have all sides and axes the same length, and all would meet each other at right angles. A model for the *triclinic* system is a bit more complex, since it requires sides and axes of different lengths, all meeting at angles that are not right angles.

Once you've constructed the models, you may want to spray paint them to make them more eyecatching. Also, you might want to distinguish the models' axes from the sides by hand-painting the axes a different color after the spray paint job is dry. Remember: if you use match sticks, remove and discard their flammable tips before you build your models. Once the models are complete, use 3 by 5 cards to label each by its name and its distinguishing characteristics. Also list one or more minerals that are examples of the system. Figure 4-5 shows a sample label.

Linking Mineralogy with Everyday Life: An Exhibit of Common Minerals Found at Home

Information Needed:	☐ The Mineral Identification Table (Figure 3-10)
Equipment:	☐ Common mineral substances found about your home
	☐ A specimen tray
	☐ 3 by 5 cards
	☐ A magnifying glass

a model of
the hexagonal crystal system

— it contains four axes
— three axes are the same length; one is different
— three axes meet at 120°; the other one meets them at 90°

examples of minerals in the hexagonal crystal system: beryl, calcite, cinnabar, quartz, tourmaline

Figure 4-5. *A descriptive card for a crystal system model*

This is a wonderfully simple yet informative display featuring common household substances that are excellent examples of important minerals. These can be found in the kitchen, at the dinner table, and even in the bathroom. **Be sure to read all labels.** Keep in mind that some of these substances, such as chemical drain openers, are potentially very dangerous and should not be handled or included in the display.

Perhaps the best known of the safe everyday minerals is found in your salt shaker. Place some of the salt on your specimen tray and use a 3 by 5 card to label it. The magnifying glass will allow you to see the distinct crystal structure of its tiny grains. Other mineral samples should also be placed or mounted on the specimen tray.

And, come to think of it, how many other minerals can you collect for the exhibit? Here are some hints:

What about the tips of pencils, baking soda, or the contents of a sandbox? Do you have any copper wire lying about, or any borax soap, or any calcite in the form of limestone driveway gravel? You may be surprised by the number of common but significant minerals you end up with!

THE WORLD OF ROCKS

Collecting and Classifying:
Prospecting for Rocks

Information Needed:	☐ The location of accessible rock outcrops
	☐ A geological bedrock map of your state or area, showing the names and ages of rock formations (not available for all locations)
	☐ A field guide to rocks
	☐ A boxed rock set (optional)
Field Equipment:	☐ A rock hammer
	☐ A crowbar or rock pick (optional)
	☐ Safety glasses or other protective eyewear
	☐ Heavy-duty collection bags
	☐ A field notebook
	☐ A marking pen
Other Supplies:	☐ A display box, tray, or shelf for your specimens
	☐ Sample labels
	☐ 3 by 5 cards
	☐ A 3 by 5 card file box
	☐ White enamel model paint
	☐ Red enamel model paint
	☐ A model paintbrush and a sewing needle

This activity is one that is familiar to many geologists: a search for good rock samples, followed by their identification, first by their basic groups, then by their exact types.

Rock prospecting is much the same as mineral hunting, except that rock outcrops are almost always easier to find than suitable mineral samples. Once again, you should collect only where permitted. Be especially careful: watch out for falling rocks, and keep out of the way of traffic at roadside locations.

Although rock outcrops may be plentiful, collection-quality rock specimens may be a little harder to obtain than you would expect. First of all, you must be sure that your specimens *do* come from the outcrop you want, and aren't just loose stones that have been moved from some other source, far away. Also, many rock outcrops, when exposed to the elements, eventually become stained with chemical residues known as *weathering*. Since weathering usually hides or changes a rock's true appearance, it's very important to take samples with at least one or two fresh sides. If necessary, use your rock hammer to split apart a rock totally covered with weathering. When you do so, check to see that it isn't "rotten," or weathered all the way through. Generally, you will find the freshest outcrop samples lie behind the exposed surface of stone, so you may have to do some coaxing and prying. Flying rock chips and splinters are a real possibility, so wear safety glasses or goggles.

As you gather your rock specimens, keep the samples from each location separate, and write good field notes so you won't forget exactly when and where you got the specimens. Also record the appearance of the outcrop itself. Were there several rock types present there, or just one? Were the rocks arranged in distinct layers? Were there any fossils or special minerals that may help identify the units later?

When you return home, review your field notes, then determine which overall rock group (or groups) your samples belong to. Review the description of igneous, sedimentary, and metamorphic rocks in Chapter Three, then refer to your field guide.

Once you've done this, you can proceed with a more detailed analysis. For example, if you've found a sample in a layered rock formation and know it's definitely sedimentary, you can then check each of the sedimentary rocks—conglomerate, sandstone, shale, limestone, and so on—to see which kind fits the best. When you have identified your specimens, number them with model paint, using the same method for mineral samples shown in Figure 4-1. Then make display labels similar to the one illustrated by Figure 4-6. (You may find that you prefer another kind of label. Always experiment and use what suits you best.)

Finally, record the important information about each sample on 3 by 5 cards that can be kept in a file box. You may want to use the kind of format shown in Figure 4-7.

One last note about identifying your rock samples: You can verify your findings by consulting a bedrock geology map, if one has been published for your state or local area. Such a map will give you the names, ages, and extent of rock formations you've seen.

Experimenting:
Mapping Rock Types and
Interpreting the Results

Information Needed:	☐ Your rock specimen card file
Equipment:	☐ A U.S. Geological Survey topographic quadrangle map of your area, mounted on a cork board or cardboard
	☐ Stickpins of different colors

In this activity several points are especially important. You must collect and identify rock outcrop samples from

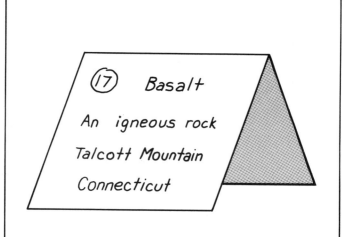

Figure 4-6. *A label for a rock specimen*

rock specimen no. 17

collection site:	Talcott Mountain, Connecticut —at a summit outcrop just north of Heublein Tower
collection date:	28 June 1991
general rock type:	igneous
specific rock type:	basalt (also known as "traprock")
geologic age:	Jurassic Period, about 200 million years ago
other information:	Talcott Mountain is one of several traprock ridges in this state. The basalt was originally a lava flow.

Figure 4-7. *A specimen card from a rock collection file*

a number of locations within the area covered by one topographic map. In fact, using ten, fifteen, or even more sampling sites is preferable. This means you'll be involved in more than one trip or one day's fieldwork. It's also essential to take outcrop samples from both high ground (hills, hummocks, ridges, or mountains) and low ground (valley bottoms, streambeds, or washes) and to find and record each rock type in more than one place. Take along a copy of the topographic map, and determine the exact location of each sampling site while you're there. If the map is hard to understand, ask a teacher or other knowledgeable adult to explain it to you before you go.

When your fieldwork is done, number your new samples and update your rock collection card file. Then use the updated information to determine how many different rock types you actually found in the map area. Next, assign each kind of rock its own color of pins, and place the pins in the map where you found your specimens. For instance, if you find basalt, shale, and sandstone in the map area, you can place a black pin at each location on the map where you find the basalt, a red pin for each sandstone site, and a green pin every place you found the shale.

Now you're ready to assemble the bits of information, or *data*, that you gathered in the field. Using the previous example, you may find that the black basalt pins occur on the map only on hilltops, while the green shale pins are mostly in the valleys, with the red sandstone in between, on middle ground. If so, you've discovered an important pattern. Since the high places have resisted erosion more successfully than the low areas, it stands to reason that the basalt (in this region, at least) is harder to erode than the sandstone or shale.

By plotting different rock types on a map, and seeing how they reflect the shape of the land, you are performing one important kind of research undertaken by geologists. Interpretation of your mapping always involves lots of guesswork, but if you're careful you can make exciting discoveries about your own landscape. In addition, you can use the results of this mapping experiment to create an interesting display that includes a description of which rocks resist erosion better than others.

Illustrating Interesting Shapes in Nature: Rocks with Different Forms

Information Needed:	☐ A field guide to rocks
Equipment:	☐ A collection of rock specimens of different shapes
	☐ A large specimen tray or display table
	☐ 3 by 5 cards or other labels for your rock specimens

Rocks can be compared and classified in more than one way. This project illustrates that point. Instead of making a display collection of rocks based on their sedimentary, igneous, or metamorphic origin, you can group rocks by their overall shape. For example, smooth, rounded cobbles, such as those found in a streambed or on the beach, can make up one main grouping, while sharp-edged or rough-textured samples can constitute another.

The key to this project is to be as imaginative as possible. When you label each rock specimen you may wish to speculate on the geologic forces that gave it its present shape. The streambed cobble was clearly smoothed by the force of running water, for instance, and some pitted volcanic rocks owe their rough, irregular surface to gas bubbles that were present in the cooling lava that became the rock. From this you may be able to draw more general conclusions: are smooth rocks always the result of flowing water, or could some other force achieve the same results? And are volcanic rocks uniformly harsh to the touch, or can some have slick surfaces?

Highlighting Your Local Lithology: Assembling an Assortment of Rocks of Your Own State

Information Needed:	☐ A field guide to rocks
	☐ The bedrock geology map of your state, if available, or the AAPG Geological Highway Map of the region that includes your state (optional)
Equipment:	☐ A collection of rock specimens found in your state, placed in a display box or tray
	☐ 3 by 5 cards or other labels for the rocks in your display
	☐ Posterboard or stout cardboard, for one poster
	☐ A map of your state (a road map is fine)
	☐ Colored stick pins
	☐ Rubber cement or glue for paper

This activity complements the similar project on the minerals of your state, described earlier. In this case, however, you make only a single poster. Do so by carefully mounting the state map on the cardboard or posterboard with glue. Then trim the edges of the poster as necessary.

Since samples of stone are often larger and heavier than mineral specimens, set your rocks in a display box or tray rather than trying to glue them to a poster that will have to stand upright. Label the rock specimens by listing their type—limestone, basalt, gneiss, or whatever—and by noting the places they occur in your state. If you know the geologic ages of the specimens, or the names of the formations from which they came, make sure you put them down, too.

Once again, you have a choice of how you can use the map poster. You can use stick pins to show exactly where the rock specimens were collected, or you can point out where larger formations of bedrock occur. To find out more, obtain the AAPG highway map or a bedrock geology map that covers your entire state.

Explaining the Three Main Rock Groups: A Display on How They Are Created

Information Needed:	☐ The description of the three main rock groups, in Chapter Three.
Equipment:	☐ Two or three representative rock specimens for each of the three rock groups
	☐ Three separate rock trays, one for each of the rock groups
	☐ 3 by 5 cards or other labels for the rock specimens
	☐ Three pieces of posterboard, suitable for the drawing of diagrams
	☐ Colored marker pens

While its main objective may seem straightforward enough, this activity calls for some extra researching—and also for good hand printing or drafting of diagrams. If you have an artistic bent you'll be able to turn this highly informative project into a real showpiece.

Begin by arranging your igneous rock samples in one specimen tray, your sedimentary samples in another, and your metamorphic specimens in yet another. Use labels to indicate which rock group is represented by which box. Then label each individual rock by listing its exact type (sandstone, gabbro, schist, and so on), and if possible note where it was collected.

Next, the graphics. For each specimen box make a poster of your design to explain, in simple terms, how each rock type came into being. For instance, suppose your igneous rock sample box contains basalt lava, the volcanic glass called obsidian, and granite. You may draw a cross section of the earth's crust, complete with a volcano. You can show that (1) the granite formed far below the surface, (2) the obsidian formed aboveground near the volcano's vent, and (3) the basalt lava originated in a surface flow some distance from the volcano.

If you prefer writing descriptions rather than drawing them, you can print brief explanations on the poster instead. Use block letters and different colored markers for each rock description. To pick a single item from your sedimentary sample collection, you can describe how sandstone is deposited by wind or streams in lowland areas or just offshore. For your metamorphic box, you may have a piece of marble that can be described on the poster as limestone and has been transformed by intense pressure or increased temperature. To understand how each individual rock type originated, you may wish to consult additional geology books that deal with the subject in greater detail. These books can be found in your school or town library.

Linking Rocks with the History of the Earth: A Geologic Timescale Poster

Information Needed:	☐ The description of the geologic timescale in Chapter Three
	☐ A geologic bedrock map of your state, preferably one that lists the names of rock formations
Equipment:	☐ Posterboard or stout cardboard for one 36 by 24 poster
	☐ A soft-leaded pencil
	☐ Colored marking pens
	☐ Model paint or labels to number your rock specimens

As noted elsewhere in this book, the geologic timescale is one of the most important concepts in earth science. This project is one way to introduce others to the vast length of geologic time, and to show them the great age of rocks collected in your region.

Using our discussion and illustrations of the geologic timescale as your guide, create your own version of it on a blank geologic timescale poster (see chapter One). Remember that space on the poster is limited, so don't get too detailed. Begin by lightly penciling in the eras: the Precambrian, Paleozoic, Mesozoic, and Cenozoic.

Before you do the finished version of the timescale, turn to your rock collection and your state bedrock geology map. Number your rock specimens with paint or labels, and then match them one by one with the names of the rock formations they came from, as shown on the map. For example, suppose you collected a beautiful piece of green metamorphic rock, known as serpentine, from an outcrop located in the town of Rochester, Vermont. You would locate Rochester on the Vermont bedrock map, then match the color and symbols shown for the rock formation present in that town with the color and symbol shown on the map's legend. If it says that the serpentine in Rochester is from the Pinney Hollow Formation of the Cambrian Period, you can annotate your poster's timescale with an arrow and the appropriate specimen number to show that your serpentine comes from the Cambrian Period, at the very beginning of the Paleozoic Era. Determine the age of each of the other rock specimens in the same way, and annotate them too on the timescale poster.

Don't expect that your rock collection will represent rocks from all the geologic eras. A few states, such as Arizona, are blessed with rock outcrops ranging from very ancient to very recent, but in most cases your rock samples will cover a relatively small slice of time. Regardless of what formation or era your rocks come from, they're bound to provoke curiosity when they're linked to the overall history of the earth.

THE WORLD OF FOSSILS

Collecting and Classifying:
Searching for Fossils

Information Needed:	☐ The location of good fossil collecting sites (the AAPG *Geological Highway Map* for your region lists many of these sites)
	☐ A field guide to fossils
	☐ A boxed fossil collection (optional)
Field Equipment:	☐ A rock hammer
	☐ A crowbar or rock pick (optional)
	☐ Safety glasses or other protective eyewear
	☐ A roll of bathroom tissue, for wrapping fossils
	☐ Collection bags
	☐ A field notebook
	☐ A marking pen
Other Supplies:	☐ A display box, tray, or shelf for your specimens
	☐ Sample labels
	☐ 3 by 5 cards
	☐ A 3 by 5 card file box
	☐ White enamel model paint
	☐ Red enamel model paint
	☐ A model paintbrush and a sewing needle
	☐ A biology probe for cleaning fossil surfaces (a sewing needle taped to the end of a stick can be used instead)
	☐ A toothbrush (this also is for fossil cleaning)

We begin this activity with a simple reminder: with very rare exceptions, fossils occur only in sedimentary rocks. On top of that, many sedimentary formations contain few if any fossils. So it's best to find out ahead of time what rockbeds in your region are most likely to reward your search. Even when you've located an outcrop that is a sure bet, you may have to hunt patiently for hours before you make your first find. And as always, you should obtain permission as necessary before you visit each collection site.

When you're ready to start your hunt at a likely outcrop, loosen chunks of rock from the rock face, then carefully split them open by prying them with a crowbar or rock pick or by tapping them with your rock hammer. (Once again, don't forget your goggles or safety glasses.) Rocks often split along the fossil surface, to reveal an inner portion, called the *cast,* and an outer portion, the *mold.*

Fossils are often fragile. To lessen the chance of breakage, wrap all specimens in bathroom tissue before you put them in your collection bag. Later on, when you return home, you'll be able to clean dust and rock fragments away with delicate instruments such as the biology probe and toothbrush.

The process of preparing fossils for a collection is similar to that of preparing rocks or minerals. Fossils can be numbered in the method depicted in Figure 4-1. You may wish to classify your specimens by the types of plant or animal they are; your field guide will be one good source of information, but you may have to look through museum exhibits, textbooks, and other publications to discover the exact identity of some samples. If you need help finding this information, ask your school librarian or a science teacher.

Another interesting way to classify your fossils is by their age. Some creatures—trilobites, for instance—are found in rocks of several geologic periods. You can determine their exact place in the history of the earth by finding the age of their rock formations, as shown on a geologic bedrock map.

Labels for your fossil specimens should contain information about their identity, geologic period, and place of discovery (Figure 4-8). In the same way, your card file listing for a particular fossil in your collection may look something like Figure 4-9.

Experimenting:
Determining Ancient Environments

Information
Needed:

☐ Fossil specimens from your collection

☐ Your fossil information card file

☐ A field guide to fossils
Other information on fossils (discussed later)

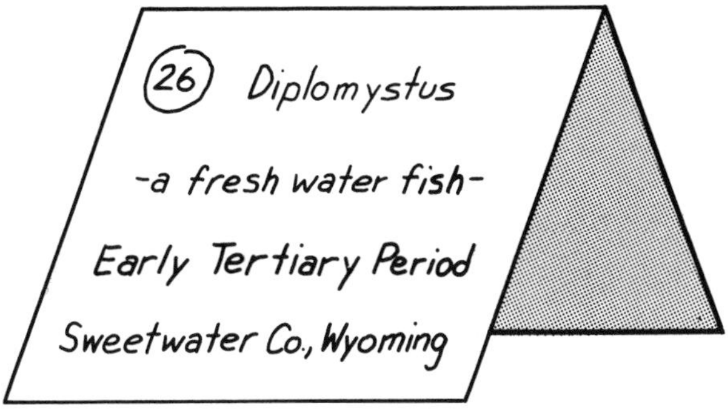

Figure 4-8. *A label for a fossil specimen*

```
┌─────────────────────────────────────────────────┐
│  ┌───────────────────────────────────────────┐  │
│  │                                           │  │
│  │         fossil specimen no. 26            │  │
│  │                                           │  │
│  │  collection site:      outcrop in Sweetwater Co., Wyoming  │
│  │  collection date:      17 October 1992    │  │
│  │  name of fossil:       Diplomystus         │  │
│  │  type of fossil:       fresh water fish    │  │
│  │  rock formation name:  Green River formation │
│  │  rock formation age:   early Tertiary Period │
│  │  comments:             an unusual kind of fossil—created │
│  │                        by volcanic ash falling on an │
│  │                        inland lake        │  │
│  │                                           │  │
│  └───────────────────────────────────────────┘  │
│                                                 │
│  Figure 4-9.   A specimen card from a fossil    │
│  collection file                                │
│                                                 │
└─────────────────────────────────────────────────┘
```

Paleontologists and other kinds of geologists often find fossils useful for more than one reason. Not only do fossils help determine the exact ages of rock formations—they also tell us much about the different environments that existed in a particular place, when the creatures they represent were still living. And that is the purpose of this activity. By analyzing your fossil specimens, you will learn more about how the earth has changed in the long course of geologic time.

A crucial step in any scientific experiment is the *interpretation of the evidence.* In this case, your evidence is your fossil collection. To interpret it correctly, you must hunt for suggestions and clues about its significance. In other words, you need more information than the identity of the specimens themselves.

Your field guide to fossils is one obvious source of more information about your fossils, but don't forget the other resources mentioned in the previous section—the museum exhibits, publications, and so on. These will give you a clearer picture of the world each creature lived in.

Let's take a look at how your interpretation of the evidence might proceed. For example, imagine you have collected two fossils from two different rock layers at one outcrop. The first specimen is a part of a leaf from a seed fern tree known as *Pecopteris*. From your picture guide and other books you've learned that this tree lived in swampy lowlands in the Pennsylvanian Period, roughly 300 million years ago.

The second specimen was an animal, a brachiopod named *Mucrospirifer*. At first you can't find out much about it, but then your science teacher suggests you contact the local nature museum. Sure enough, your patient research finally pays off. Someone at the museum finds a book on paleontology that describes *Mucrospirifer*. As it turns out, it lived on the bottom of shallow seas in the Devonian Period, about 50 million years before the *Pecopteris* tree existed.

From these two fossils you can reconstruct what the collection site was like at two widely separated points in the earth's history. Your interpretation demonstrates that what is a rock outcrop on dry land now was once a tropical swamp, and even before that, an ocean!

Illustrating a Vanished World: Making a Diorama That Shows a Fossil's Original Habitat and Surroundings

Information Needed:	☐ A field guide to fossils
	☐ A paleontology picture book that shows ancient environments
Equipment:	☐ A fossil from your collection
	☐ A 3 by 5 card or other label for your fossil specimen
	☐ A cardboard shoebox or similar container

□ Modeling clay

□ Construction paper, pipe cleaners, drinking straws, and other materials you choose for the diorama interior

□ A box of clear kitchen wrap

□ Colored drawing pens

□ Model glue, model paints, and a modeling paintbrush

This project is a good follow-on activity to the preceding experimenting section. If you've ever visited a natural history museum, you've probably seen a *diorama*, or model of a particular setting of special interest. Some dioramas show early human beings hunting Ice Age prey or standing in family groups beside their shelters. Others portray animals from other parts of the world against the backdrop of their own landscape and vegetation.

Your goal here is to select one of your fossil specimens and to recreate the environment it occupied when it was a living being. The previous project gives you some ideas how to do the research to find out what kind of habitat your fossil inhabited. When you have a good idea of what the habitat was and you have a good mental picture of what you want to show, prepare the shoebox to serve as the diorama chamber.

First remove the shoebox top and cut away one of the longer sides of the shoebox, so that you'll have a large viewing window. Make sure that you don't remove the box's bottom by mistake! Then use colored marking pens to illustrate the insides of the three remaining walls. Don't hesitate to use your imagination, but remember that the pictures on the walls should represent things in the distance, in the background of your fossil's habitat. For instance, if you're illustrating a coal swamp of the Pennsylvanian Period, you'll probably want all sorts of trees in the background, but they should be smaller than those you'll make in the front of the diorama.

When you have finished the background, use the modeling clay to make a small figure of the plant or animal represented by your fossil specimen. For added realism, paint the figure the color or colors you think it was in real life. (If you're not sure, go ahead and choose something plausible. Your guess may be as good as the experts!) Next, use the clay and the other construction materials to represent other objects or creatures in the foreground. All objects in the foreground will have to be secured by gluing them to the floor of the box to prevent damage.

When you're satisfied with the way the diorama interior looks, attach clear kitchen wrap to cover the front viewing window, and then replace the shoebox top. If the diorama interior is too dark to see when the top is on, you can cut light holes or slits in the top. If these holes are large, you may want to protect them with a covering of clear kitchen wrap, as well. A sample diorama is shown in Figure 4-10.

Highlighting Your Local Paleontology:
Assembling an Assortment of Fossils
of Your Own State

Information Needed:	☐ A field guide to fossils
	☐ A bedrock geology map of your state
Equipment:	☐ A collection of fossils found in your state, placed in a display box or tray
	☐ 3 by 5 cards or other labels for the fossils in your display
	☐ Posterboard or stout cardboard, for one poster
	☐ A map of your state (a road map is fine)
	☐ Colored stick pins
	☐ Rubber cement or glue for paper

Figure 4-10. *An example of a diorama, showing a Paleozoic Era seafloor scene*

Many people think fossils are exotic objects that come from remote places. This exhibit shows that the remains of ancient life can often be found quite close to home. There are a few places—such as New Hampshire, the Granite State—where fossils are very rare indeed, but most states have at least some fossil-bearing rock formations.

To create your display, label each of the fossil specimens by giving its name, its geologic age, and the place and rock formation from which it was collected. If you're not sure of the formation's name or age, check a bedrock geology map for your state.

The next step is to glue your state roadmap on the poster board and to cut away any excess board from the edges. Place the colored pins to show where your fossils were found. If you wish, you can also use stickpins or labels to indicate where other important fossil sites are located in the state. In addition, you may want to highlight the locations of museums or universities where major fossil collections are on public display.

Explaining How Fossils Come into Being:
A Display of the Different Types
of Preservation

Information Needed:	☐ A field guide to fossils or a paleontology book that describes the various ways fossils are preserved
Equipment:	☐ A collection of fossils that illustrate different types of preservation, placed in separate display boxes
	☐ Enough posterboard or stout cardboard for one 12 by 8 poster for each fossil specimen
	☐ Colored marking pens

Not all fossils are created equal. If you've gone fossil-hunting in a limestone quarry where the remains of crinoids, brachiopods, and other invertebrate sea creatures are abundant, you know that some specimens have survived the test of time better than others. Just a few inches from one fossil that is barely distinguishable you may find one that has almost every detail superbly preserved. And on top of that, different kinds of fossils vary in the *way* they were preserved. That is the theme of this project: to display and explain some of the various physical and chemical processes that work to preserve characteristics of long-vanished forms of life.

Naturally, before you can set up this exhibit you have to understand what the most common modes of fossil preservation are. In other words, you'll want to research the subject by referring to a book on general paleontology that discusses the matter in some detail. At the very least, make sure you're familiar with these kinds of preservation:

1. *The retention of an organism's hard parts,* as in the case of sharks' teeth or animal bones that survive intact

2. *Permineralization,* which involves the petrification of an organism as minerals are partially absorbed into its hard parts

3. *Replacement,* which involves the petrification of an organism as minerals completely replace the original hard parts

4. *Molds* and *casts,* which are produced from organisms leaving impressions in soft sediments that are later filled in to produce inner and outer forms of the fossil

5. *Carbonization,* in which the original tissue (especially that of plants) is reduced to a thin carbon film.

If you don't have examples of each of these types of fossilization, try to obtain pictures of the missing types for your display. For each fossil specimen or illustration you have, prepare a poster which describes its mode of preservation. You may find that you can describe each example best by using a straight written text in block letters—or you may discover that you're better at explaining things with a combination of words and simple drawings. As with all the other activities in this section, the key to success lies in trying out different approaches, till you find the one that works best.

Linking Fossils with Continental Drift: Mapping Wandering Lands and Their Life-Forms through Space and Time

Information Needed:

☐ An artist's rendering of continental drift from a geology text as it occurred through the various eras, starting with the Cambrian

☐ A field guide to fossils

☐ A bedrock geology map for the locations where you collected your fossils (optional)

Equipment:	☐ Two or three good fossil specimens
	☐ An inexpensive map of the world, or a globe of the earth, at least 12 inches in diameter
	☐ Posterboard or stout cardboard (not needed if you use a globe instead of a world map)
	☐ Rubber cement or glue for paper (not needed if you use a globe)
	☐ Stickpins and string of several colors *or* thin (⅛ inch) artist's highlighting tape of several colors (the tape is better than stickpins and string, especially if you use a globe instead of a map)

For many years geologists believed that our continent, along with the other great landmasses of the world, was permanently fixed to its own place on the earth's exterior. Only in the last few decades has it become clear that continents move—though very, very slowly—around our planet's surface.

One important tool earth scientists use to uncover the secrets of continental drift is the fossil record itself. By comparing similar fossils that exist on two continents now widely separated by an ocean, paleontologists can determine that those two pieces of land were once joined in a different place, back when the fossils were still living organisms. In fact, a sea lily fossil found today in an Indiana outcrop may have traveled northward thousands of miles, from a starting point below the equator! Of course, it could only travel that far because it was a part of our moving continent for millions upon millions of years.

This activity is an especially good one for science fairs or school exhibits because it links something tangible—your fossil specimens—with one of the greatest theories of modern geology—continental drift. To begin, you must be sure of the geologic age of your fossils. If you don't already know what periods they are from, match them with the appropriate descriptions in a field guide to fossils. If that doesn't help, check a bedrock geology map to determine the age of the rock formations in which they were found.

Once you've determined the age of each fossil, find the continental drift diagram for your specimen's geologic period. (For example, if you have an Ordovician Period sea lily fossil, find an Ordovician diagram.) Then, locate your specimen's original location on the ancient version of North America. Let's say that your fossil does come from Indiana. You approximate as best you can where Indiana is situated on the Ordovician diagram, and then note which latitude and longitude lines lie closest to that position. If you need assistance finding the position or understanding the latitude and longitude lines, ask a parent or teacher to help you.

The next part involves your world map or globe. If you decide to use a map, carefully mount it on a poster backing with rubber cement or paper glue. Once you're done with that, match the ancient location of your fossil as shown on the continental drift diagram with corresponding longitude and latitude lines on your globe or modern world map. To show you how that's done, let's continue with our Indiana example. In the Ordovician Period that state was located below the equator, south of where it is now. So you place a stick pin or an erasable dot in that location on the map or globe, even though it may now point to a part of the Pacific Ocean or another landmass. Then you use another pin or dot to mark the *modern* location of Indiana. When you connect these two pins or dots with colored string or highlighting tape, you are showing the distance the continent has traveled since the fossil was a living animal in the Ordovician Period. Figure 4-11 illustrates the distance line as plotted on both a map and a globe.

If you're lucky enough to have two or three fossils from different states and different geologic periods, you

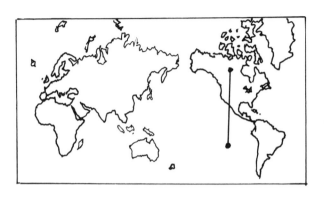

Figure 4-11. *Continental drift distance lines plotted on both a map poster and on a globe*

should come up with three distinct colored distance lines on your globe or map. If your fossils are all from the same time and place, however, the distance lines will all be identical. In that case, you may want to use renderings of well-known fossil types from other points in the geologic timescale. If you already have an Ordovician sea lily, you can supplement it with a drawing of a Jurassic Period dinosaur and a photograph of a Pennsylvanian Period seed fern fossil. Even though you don't have actual specimens of the seed fern or the dinosaur, you can use the same method and determine their distance lines, too.

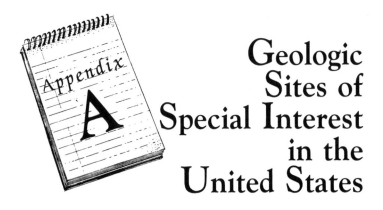

Geologic Sites of Special Interest in the United States

The United States is a nation extremely rich in geologic treasures. Each section of the country boasts many first-rate sites—and on top of that it's quite likely that you'll find something of great interest close to home.

The following locations, listed region by region, are just the beginning of the list. With a little additional research you will find many other places worth investigating. One good place to learn more about our nation's geologic treasures is your area's National Park Service headquarters. There you can obtain a brochure that includes a comprehensive list of all national parks and monuments. Also, you can check with the government agency that administers your own state's parks. In all likelihood its headquarters are located in the state capital.

1. THE NORTHEAST

Eastern New York and the New England states abound in mineral and gemstone collecting localities, while much of New York, along with the Connecticut River Valley of Massachusetts and Connecticut, is a prime fossil-hunting territory.

Since the Northeast has many large cities, there are many museums to visit. Among the most appealing to geologists are the American Museum of Natural History in New York City; the Peabody Museum of Yale University in New Haven, Connecticut; and the Pratt Museum in Amherst, Massachusetts. Vermont has two wonderful quarry exhibits: in the marble center of Proctor, and in Barre, which is world-famous for its granite.

There are also numerous attractions outdoors. Maine's breathtakingly beautiful Acadia National Park combines rugged hill and seacoast scenery with a fascinating geologic history; in Connecticut, a dramatic display of ancient reptile footprints is preserved at Dinosaur State Park. The Cape Cod National Seashore in Massachusetts is an excellent place to learn more about beaches, sand dunes, and the Ice Age, and the well-known Niagara Falls near Buffalo, New York, is one of North America's greatest natural spectacles. New Hampshire's magnificent Mount Washington is the tallest mountain in the Northeast, as well as one of the best places to see the work of past glaciers.

2. THE MID-ATLANTIC STATES

In this region gemstones and other minerals are most common in northern Delaware, eastern Pennsylvania, and northern New Jersey. Fossils are found in rock units in eastern West Virginia, northern Delaware, and southern Pennsylvania. Museums with earth science exhibits include the Smithsonian Institution in Washington, D.C., the Philadelphia Academy of Science, and the Mineral Museum in Franklin, New Jersey.

Several Atlantic Coast sites, such as Cape Henlopen State Park in Delaware and Sandy Hook State Park in New Jersey, are ideal places to study the movement of sediments borne by ocean waves and currents. Moraine State Park in Pennsylvania displays several intriguing Ice Age landforms, and you can see a great river that has cut through a towering hillside at the magnificent Delaware Water Gap, on the boundary between Pennsylvania and New Jersey.

3. THE SOUTHEAST

Fossil corals are plentiful in Florida, petrified wood occurs in Mississippi and Louisiana, and there are other good fossil sites in northern Kentucky, western Tennessee, and the eastern sections of Virginia, North Carolina, and South Carolina. As far as minerals and gemstones go, the northern parts of Georgia and Alabama are a good bet, as are western North Carolina and the central portions of Virginia and Kentucky.

Several museums are of special note. You can see the Hodges Meteorite and other geologic attractions at the University of Alabama Museum of Natural History in Tuscaloosa; another big attraction is the Louisiana State University Museum of Geoscience and Natural History in Baton Rouge.

Kentucky's famous Mammoth Cave National Park contains stalactites, stalagmites, and other amazing limestone cavern features, while Stone Mountain, outside Atlanta, is a lonely prominence of granite with a commanding view of the surrounding Georgia landscape. North Carolina's Mount Mitchell State Park contains the highest point in the eastern United States, and the Mississippi Petrified Forest near Flora offers a self-guiding trail and examples of ancient plant life.

4. THE MIDWEST

Every state in this region contains good fossil-collecting sites; mineral and gemstone hunting is particularly good in Wisconsin, Michigan's Upper Peninsula, and the northwestern part of Illinois. Geology exhibits may be found at Chicago's famous Field Museum and at the Illinois State Museum in Springfield, as well as at the

121

Cleveland and Cincinnati natural history museums, and the Indiana State Museum in Indianapolis.

There are also many outstanding natural areas. The Indiana Dunes National Lakeshore, at the southern tip of Lake Michigan, features huge, slowly migrating hills of sand; at scenic Devil's Lake State Park in Wisconsin you can see a large body of water dammed by debris left behind by retreating glaciers. Illinois's Starved Rock State Park is an excellent place to see sedimentary strata, and Isle Royale National Park, in Lake Superior, has out-crops of rocks formed by volcanoes more than a billion years ago, long before plants and animals invaded the land.

5. THE NORTH CENTRAL STATES

The mining district of northeastern Minnesota is a prime site for mineral collectors; other minerals and gem-stones may be found in eastern Iowa, northern Ne-braska, as well as the western parts of both the Dakotas. Fossil-hunting grounds in this region range from south-western North Dakota to southeastern Minnesota, and from southern Nebraska to eastern Iowa.

There are a number of interesting public areas, from Mount Rushmore and the unearthly Badlands National Monument, both in South Dakota, to Minnesota's Pipestone National Monument, Nebraska's Agate Fossil Beds National Monument, and Iowa's Preparation Can-yon State Park (where you can see unusual hills formed from windblown silt). You also may wish to visit the Geology Department Museum at the University of North Dakota at Grand Forks, or the A. M. Chisholm Mu-seum in Duluth, Minnesota. And, if you'd like to learn more about how satellites and aircaft are used to study the earth, visit the EROS Data Center located north of Sioux Falls, South Dakota.

6. THE SOUTH CENTRAL STATES

Texas fossil sites are found in the central and western portions of the state; also check out eastern Missouri, southwestern Arkansas, and southern Oklahoma. Gemstones and minerals are most common in northeastern Kansas, eastern Oklahoma, eastern Missouri, and much of Arkansas and Texas.

If you are a mineral collector, don't miss Crater of Diamonds State Park in Arkansas—if you're very, very lucky you may even find a diamond of your own. If, on the other hand, you're more interested in learning about fossils, canyons, or volcanic formations, the remote but awesomely beautiful Big Bend National Park in western Texas should be a top priority. Hahatonka State Park in Missouri features natural bridges and sinkholes, while Oklahoma's Alabaster Caverns State Park has unique gypsum caves. In addition, the University of Kansas at Lawrence has a Museum of Natural History, with geology exhibits.

7. THE ROCKY MOUNTAIN STATES

As you might expect, the Rockies region is a geologic treasure chest. Collecting areas for minerals and gemstones, and for fossils, too, abound in all the states— Montana, Wyoming, Colorado, Utah, and Idaho.

Some of the biggest fossils you're likely to see are on display at Dinosaur National Monument in Colorado—and the Denver Museum of Natural History is one of the very best. This region boasts some of the most geologically fascinating national parks: Yellowstone and Grand Teton in Wyoming, Rocky Mountain in Colorado, Glacier in Montana, and Zion, Arches, Canyonlands, and Bryce Canyon in Utah. As if that weren't enough, extinct volcanoes can be seen at the Craters of the Moon National Monument in Idaho, and magnificent scenery and dramatic sedimentary rock units are found at Colorado National Monument near Grand Junction.

8. THE SOUTHWEST

The Southwest contains some of the richest fossil- and mineral-hunting locales, many of which are in the western half of New Mexico and southeastern Arizona.

This part of the country is unsurpassed in its beauty, and it has some of the most famous public lands in America. In Arizona alone, the privately administered Meteor Crater demonstrates the power of a meteorite hitting the earth's surface in fairly recent times; Petrified Forest National Park is a showcase of giant fossilized tree trunks over 200 million years old; and at Grand Canyon National Park you can get the one best geology lesson available anywhere. Not to be outdone, New Mexico has Carlsbad Caverns National Park and White Sands National Monument, and Nevada has the stark grandeur of Great Basin National Park.

9. THE PACIFIC COAST

Fossils are found in many places in California, as well as the western sections of both Oregon and Washington. Gemstones and minerals are even more broadly distributed throughout much of these three states.

A number of natural history museums, such as the San Francisco Academy of Sciences, feature geology exhibits. Outdoor wonders are plentiful, too: Yosemite National Park and Lassen Volcanic National Park in California, Crater Lake National Park in Oregon, and Olympic National Park, Mount Rainier National Park, and Ginkgo Petrified Forest State Park in Washington.

Sources
for
Maps

For topographic maps and for some state geologic maps, write to

> Distribution Branch
> U.S. Geological Survey
> Box 25286, Federal Center
> Denver, CO 80225

For AAPG Geological Highway Maps for all regions of the United States contact

> American Association of
> Petroleum Geologists
> P.O. Box 979
> Tulsa, OK 74101

Sources for Field Equipment and Laboratory Supplies

Carolina Biological
Supply Company
2700 York Rd.
Burlington, NC 27215
(919) 584-0381

Forestry Suppliers, Inc.
P.O. Box 8397
Jackson, MS 39204-0397
(800) 647-5368

Frey Scientific Company
905 Hickory Lane
Mansfield, OH 44905
(800) 225-3739

NASCO
P.O. Box 901
Fort Atkinson, WI 53538-0901

Ward's Natural Science
Establishment
P.O. Box 92912
Rochester, NY 14692-9012
(800) 962-2660

Glossary

Ammonite: A type of extinct cephalopod mollusk that had a shell marked with sutures. Especially common in the seas of the Mesozoic Era.

Arthropod: A member of a large group of invertebrate animals which includes trilobites, crabs, insects, spiders, and scorpions. Arthropods can be identified by their segmented bodies and jointed legs.

Axis: A straight line that connects the centers of two crystal faces.

Basalt: A dark-colored, extrusive igneous rock.

Bedrock: A fixed rock formation, which may be exposed to view or covered by soil, vegetation, or sediments.

Biology probe: A laboratory tool consisting of a metal point attached to a wooden handle.

Borates: One of the mineral chemical groups. Example: borax.

Brachiopod: An invertebrate sea animal that has two valves that are not close copies of one another.

Breccia: A sedimentary rock made up of large angular fragments.

Carbonates: One of the mineral chemical groups. Examples: calcite, azurite, malachite.

Carbonization: The type of fossilization that occurs when an organism's tissue is reduced to a thin layer of carbon. Many plant fossils are preserved in this way.

Cast: A fossil in which the original organism has been dissolved away and replaced with rock material. It often resembles the structure of the original organism.

Cenozoic: The latest of the four eras of the geologic timescale. Sometimes called the "Age of the Mammals."

Cephalon: The head segment of a trilobite.

Cephalopod: A type of mollusk that includes forms common in the fossil record. Examples: ammonites, squids, and octopi.

Coal ball: An individual chunk of rock, found in coal deposits, that contains fossil plant parts.

Concretion: A round or oblong stone nodule that often contains a fossil at its center.

Conglomerate: A sedimentary rock made up of large rounded particles.

Conifer: A common type of cone-bearing plant (not including cycads). Examples: pines, spruces, redwoods.

Continental drift: The theory that continents move across the face of the earth.

Crinoid: A plantlike sea animal; a type of echinoderm. Also called *sea lily.*

Crust: The earth's uppermost layer, which rests atop the mantle.

Crystal: A solid substance that has a well-defined internal order and a characteristic shape.

Cycad: A primitive cone-bearing plant, especially prevalent in the early Mesozoic Era.

Diorama: A model of a portion of an environment or landscape.

Dolostone: A type of sedimentary rock consisting chiefly of dolomite (magnesium carbonate). It is usually formed by chemical precipitation.

Drainage net (or drainage pattern): The overall pattern formed by a river and its tributaries.

Echinoderm: A type of invertebrate sea animal. Examples: starfish, sea urchins, crinoids.

Epoch: The largest subdivision of a period on the geologic timescale.

Era: The largest subdivision of the geologic timescale.

Erosion: The wearing away of rock or soil and other sediments.

Eurypterid: A large extinct arthropod. Also called *sea scorpion.*

Extrusive rock: A type of igneous rock that forms from magma after it has erupted onto the surface of the earth.

Face: The flat surface of a crystal.

Field guide: A picture book, easily carried on trips, that helps identify minerals, rocks, fossils, or other objects or creatures.

Fieldwork: Work done outdoors.

Foliation: The layerlike alignment of crystals in metamorphic rocks.

Fossil: The remains of a past plant, animal, or other living being, found preserved in the earth's crust.

Gabbro: A dark-colored, intrusive igneous rock.

Gastropod: A type of mollusk that includes forms common in the fossil record. Examples: snails and slugs.

Geologic map: A map that shows an area's bedrock formations, or other geologic features, such as sediment deposits or glacial features.

Geologic timescale: The "planetary calendar" that spans the entire length of the earth's history. Its major subdivisions are eras, periods, and epochs.

Ginkgo: An unusual, ancient tree distantly related to the conifers. Often called a "living fossil," it has survived unchanged since the Mesozoic Era.

Gneiss: A metamorphic rock that shows foliation in the form of bands of light and dark crystals.

Granite: A common intrusive igneous rock. It is rich in silica and is usually light-colored.

Graptolite: An extinct sea animal, represented in the fossil record by thin carbon films showing branchlike structures.

Halides: One of the mineral chemical groups. Examples: rock salt, fluorite.

Hand lens: A small magnifying lens used to identify specimens in the field.

Hexagonal: One of the six crystal classes, forming a shape containing four axes—three of the same length, meeting at 120 degree angles, and one of a different length, meeting the others at right angles.

Hypothesis: A hunch or initial guess which can later be verified or refuted by experiments.

Igneous rock: Rock formed by magma cooling to solid state.

Index fossil: A fossil that helps to determine the identity or age of a particular rock unit.

Intrusive rock: A type of igneous rock formed by magma that solidifies underground.

Invertebrate: An animal that does not have a backbone. Examples: arthropods, mollusks, brachiopods, and echinoderms.

Isometric: One of the six crystal classes, forming a shape containing three axes, all the same length and all meeting at right angles.

Landform: Any feature on the earth's surface created by natural forces.

Lava: Magma that reaches the surface of the earth in a molten state.

Limestone: A type of sedimentary rock consisting chiefly of calcite (calcium carbonate) that is formed by the accumulation of remains of sea creatures, or by chemical precipitation.

Lithology: The branch of geology devoted to the study of rock types.

Magma: Molten rock beneath the earth's surface.

Mantle: The middle portion of the earth, located between the crust and the core.

Marble: Metamorphosed limestone or dolostone.

Maria (MAR-ee-a) The relatively low, flat areas on the moon's surface. The Latin word for "seas."

Mesozoic: The third era of the geologic timescale, often called the "Age of the Dinosaurs."

Metamorphic rock: Rock that is formed when sedimentary or igneous rocks are altered (but not completely melted) by geologic forces.

Mineral: A naturally occurring, nonliving, crystal-forming substance.

Mineralogy: The branch of geology devoted to the study of minerals.

Mohs Hardness Scale: A scale that rates the relative hardness of common minerals.

Mold: The impression left in surrounding rock by a shell or other organic structure.

Mollusk: A very widespread type of invertebrate animal, common in the fossil record. Examples: cephalopods, gastropods, and pelecypods.

Monoclinic: One of the six crystal classes, forming a shape containing three axes, all different lengths—two meeting at right angles, and the other meeting at less or more than a right angle.

Native elements: One of the mineral chemical groups, consisting of simple elements. Examples: carbon in the form of diamond and graphite; also gold, silver, and sulfur.

Orthorhombic: One of the six crystal classes, forming a shape containing three axes, all different lengths, and all meeting at right angles.

Outcrop: An exposed section of bedrock.

Oxides: One of the mineral chemical groups. Examples: bauxite, cuprite, and magnetite.

Paleontology: The branch of geology devoted to the study of ancient life-forms, as revealed by fossils.

Paleozoic: The second of the four eras of the geologic timescale, which included a great expansion of life in the sea and on the land.

Pangaea: The supercontinent that existed from the late Paleozoic Era to the early Mesozoic Era. It contained all the earth's major landmasses and stretched from pole to pole.

Pelecypod: A type of mollusk that has two valves that usually are close copies of one another. Examples: clams and oysters.

Period: The largest subdivision of a geologic era.

Permineralization: The type of fossilization that occurs when minerals are absorbed into an organism's hard parts.

Phosphates: One of the mineral chemical groups. Examples: apatite and turquoise.

Placoderm: A type of early armored fish that was common in the Devonian Period of the Paleozoic Era.

Plate tectonics: The theory that describes how the large pieces of the earth's crust, known as plates, move relative to one another.

Precambrian: The first and longest of the four eras of the geologic timescale begins with the creation of the earth and includes the origin of the earliest forms of life.

Pygidium: The tail section of a trilobite.

Quartzite: Metamorphosed sandstone.

Replacement: The type of fossilization that occurs when minerals take the place of an organism's original hard parts.

Rhyolite: A finely textured igneous rock. The extrusive equivalent of granite.

Roadcut: An outcrop exposed by a road excavation.

Rock hammer: A geologist's hammer, used for prying, tapping, and splitting rocks.

Rotten rock: Rock that has been weathered all the way through; often discolored and crumbly.

Sandstone: A type of sedimentary rock, formed by the accumulation and cementing together of sand particles.

Schist: A type of common metamorphic rock that shows foliation.

Scientific method: A way of learning that involves making an initial *hypothesis* about something you wish to investigate, and then testing the correctness of the hypothesis with an experiment.

Sea lily: Another name for *crinoid* (see above).

Sea scorpion: Another name for *eurypterid* (see above).

Sediments: Particles of eroded rock or other material.

Sedimentary rock: Rock formed by the accumulation of rock particles or the remains of animals or plants, or by chemical precipitation.

Shale: A type of sedimentary rock, formed by the accumulation of clay particles.

Silicates: One of the mineral chemical groups. Examples: micas, feldspars, quartz, talc, and garnet.

Slate: Metamorphosed shale.

Spoil pile: A pile of rock debris or other wastes from a mine.

Stratum: A sedimentary rock layer. The plural is *strata.*

Streak plate: A piece of unglazed porcelain used to determine the color of mineral streaks.

Sulfates: One of the mineral chemical groups. Examples: gypsum and barite.

Sulfides: One of the mineral chemical groups. Examples: cinnabar, pyrite, and galena.

Supercontinent: A giant landmass formed by the joining of two or more continents.

Suture: A marking, often resembling a complicated wavy line, found on an ammonite shell. The suture is the line along which the wall of a chamber meets the wall of the outer shell.

Tetragonal: One of the six crystal classes, forming a shape containing three axes that all meet at right angles— two the same length, and one a different length.

Thorax: The middle section of a trilobite or other arthropod.

Topographic map: A map that shows an area's landforms and their elevations.

Traprock: Another name for *basalt* (see above).

Tributary: A stream that feeds into a larger waterway, such as a major river.

Triclinic: One of the six crystal systems, forming a shape containing three axes, all of different lengths, and all meeting at angles that are not right angles.

Trilobite: An extinct type of arthropod sea animal, very widespread in the fossil record of the Paleozoic Era.

Valve: A shell part that helps to enclose the soft tissues of

brachiopods, pelecypods, and some other invertebrates.

Vertebrate: An animal that has a backbone. Examples: fishes,
amphibians, reptiles, birds, and mammals.

Weathering: The breakup of rock into simpler components.
Weathered rock is usually crumbly and discolored.

For Further Reading

FIELD GUIDES

Audubon Society Staff and Ida Thompson. *The Audubon Society Field Guide to North American Fossils.* New York: Alfred A. Knopf Company, 1982.

Chesterman, Charles W. *The Audubon Society Field Guide to North American Rocks and Minerals.* New York: Alfred A. Knopf, 1978.

Pough, Frederick H. *Rocks and Minerals* (A Peterson Field Guide). Boston, Mass.: Houghton Mifflin Company, 1983.

Rhodes, Frank T., Herbert S. Zim, and Paul R. Schaffer. *Fossils* (A Golden Nature Guide). New York: Golden Press, 1962.

Rhodes, Frank T. *Geology* (A Golden Nature Guide). New York: Golden Press, 1972.

Zim, Herbert S. and Paul R. Schaffer. *Rocks and Minerals* (A Golden Nature Guide). New York: Golden Press, 1957.

OTHER BOOKS OF INTEREST

MacFarlane, Ruth B. *Making Your Own Nature Museum.* New York: Franklin Watts, 1989. (Wonderful tips on specimen collecting and labeling.)

Roadside Geology Series. Missoula, Mont.: Mountain Press

Publishing Company. (Numerous road tour descriptions; a good way to learn geology on a trip or extended drive. Books have been published for the following states so far: Alaska, Arizona, Colorado, Idaho, Montana, New Mexico, New York, Northern California, Oregon, Pennsylvania, Texas, Utah, Vermont and New Hampshire, Virginia, and Washington.)

Shelton, John S. *Geology Illustrated.* New York: W. H. Freeman and Company, 1966. (Excellent photographs and diagrams of geologic features and processes, and step-by-step descriptions.)

Index

141

143

About
the
Author

Raymond Wiggers is Museum Editor at the Illinois State Museum in Springfield. He holds a bachelor's degree in geology from Purdue University. Mr. Wiggers has worked in a number of jobs and professions: naval officer, Environmental Protection Agency geologist, public radio announcer and program host, National Park Service ranger-naturalist, community garden planner and horticulturist, and plant-care business proprietor. He has also published *Picture Guide to Tree Leaves* with Franklin Watts. He lists his hobbies as "classical music and jazz, reading, dreaming, food, imagining things, and drawing."